Veiled

RAPTURE'S EDGE 2: Veiled

By Caris Roane

Formatting and cover by Bella Media Management.

ISBN-13: 978-1511675994

Rapture's Edge

Veiled

Episode 2
by
Caris Roane

Dear Reader,

Welcome to "Veiled", the second installment of the Rapture's Edge Series. This story is part of my Guardians of Ascension series and continues the journey of Rachel and Duncan and the black ops team of Second Earth. In many ways, each episode is a standalone story, but reading the series in order is highly recommended.

Endelle and Luken, from the original series published by St. Martin's Press, are featured prominently in the Rapture's Edge saga and each will finally find love as the series unfolds.

I chose to continue the series in an episodic form, because it was the best way to tell the ongoing journey for all my hunky Warriors of the Blood and those Militia Warriors advancing to "What-Bee" power.

"Veiled" comes right after "Awakening", a story that began the romance between Rachel and Duncan.

You'll find a terminology appendix at the end of the book in case you want to look up the meanings of a few words here and there.

"Veiled" opens one month after events in the previous episode, "Awakening", and we find Duncan and Rachel struggling to connect with each other despite Duncan's professed willingness 'to try'.

The breh-hedden (vampire mate-bonding) is still alive and well, and harassing both Duncan and Rachel, as it has all previous eight warriors so far: Kerrick, Marcus, Antony, Jean-Pierre, Thorne, Leto, Gideon, and Samuel.

Brief Synopsis of Veiled

Duncan wants to love his woman, but he's tortured by his past...

For the last few weeks, since Warrior Duncan professed his intention 'to try' to make his relationship with Rachel work, he's failed on all fronts. But how can he explain that a serpent lives in his gut, poisoning him against her? As his visions return in full-force, and the black ops team heads back to the Third Earth darkening grid, he must confront his demons or lose everything he holds dear. But will Rachel be there for him?

Rachel longs for her breh, her vampire mate, but old issues keep tearing them apart...

Rachel refuses to give up on Duncan. Though he's remained aloof because of his tortured past, she needs him more than ever. Her desire for him has reached outrageous levels as the breh-hedden continues to keep her focused solely on the man she loves. But will he finally be able to let go of his past suffering and embrace a life with her?

Caris Roane

For the *latest releases*, *hottest pics*, and *coolest contests*, be sure to sign up for my newsletter!!!

http://www.carisroane.com/contact-2/

Coming Soon: Episode #3 of RAPTURE'S EDGE, the continuing saga of the Guardians of Ascension, again featuring Duncan and Rachel. Check out RAPTURE'S EDGE on my website. http://www. carisroane.com/raptures-edge/

Coming Soon: Book #8 of the Blood Rose Series, Mastyr Ian's story: *EMBRACE THE HUNT*!!!

Be sure to check out the Blood Rose Tales Box Set – TRAPPED, HUNGER, and SEDUCED -- shorter works for a quick, sexy, satisfying read. For more information: http://www.carisroane.com/ blood-rose-tales-box-set/

Chapter One

She walks beneath a bright cloud
Hidden from all who would know her
Waiting for the unveiling
She sees him coming
A blond god of ancient Norse worlds
His arm bears a righteous sword
His eyes are lit with a holy fire
Come, she whispers
Lift the veil and know who I am
Collected Poems, **by Beatrice of Fourth**

Duncan Wallace held his wrecker shotgun in both hands, knees bent, sweating like a madman. He knew if he didn't take down the next Third grid warrior to come along, he'd be dead. He had only one advantage: Wreckers didn't see him as any kind of threat.

But where the hell was the rest of his team? They'd been running a standard grid-entry drill through the portal Merl had in his private residence. Merl had been hoping to lock onto a location on Third Earth he thought might work as a base camp for the black ops team. He'd just fired up his wrist scanner when Duncan had gotten swept somewhere else in the grid.

He didn't know what happened. One minute, he'd been standing next to Rachel and Merl, listening to the distant rumbling of wrecker warriors and waiting for them to appear. The next, he felt a soft vibration and now he was here.

He suspected Yolanthe, a Third Earth princess, was somehow involved. She'd held him in a trance for two weeks trying to bring him completely under her control. If she'd somehow found his grid signature and locked on, she could have gotten him away from the other two members of his team. But if that was true, why didn't she simply bring him straight to her?

Unless she wasn't in the grid yet. She may have moved him through an external grid operator.

Sweet Christ, he was in trouble.

He closed his eyes and took several deep breaths, as he tried to figure out what had happened and what to do next.

He reached out with his senses and focused on Yolanthe. Seconds passed, each one like a drumbeat inside his head.

The former mind-link he'd shared with Yolanthe had left a residual sense of her. He could feel the woman now, which meant if she hadn't been in the grid before, she was now. Fortunately, she was still pretty far away.

He had time, then, but not much.

He opened his eyes and glanced around. So, where was he?

Unlike Merl, he didn't have a wrist scanner, a device capable of tracking other people once inside the grid, as well as establishing a location. Only those with Third Earth powers could use it and Duncan hadn't reached Third level. For weeks now, he'd been stuck. He might have achieved Warrior of the Blood status on Second Earth, but he still couldn't access his Third gifts.

He wasn't alone since the rest of the black ops team had failed to advance as well, including Luken.

Basically, they were fucked.

He pressed himself up against the darkening grid wall, forcing himself to stay calm. At least he didn't hear the familiar distant rumbling of the wreckers. For the moment he was safe.

He contacted Rachel telepathically, wondering if he'd even be able to reach her within the grid. *Rachel, are you there?*

Duncan, thank God. I'm still with Merl, but we don't know how we got split up. He's using the grid scanner to try to locate you. What happened?

I felt a faint vibration and now I'm alone, though still in the grid. Has to be Yolanthe and I have a sense of her presence, but she's not close, at least not yet.

Hang tough. We're on it.

From the time he'd broken his mind-link with Yolanthe, she'd been working hard to pin him down and bring him back under her control. She wanted him to lead her to Rapture's Edge, though at this point he had no idea where or what it was. Although, he knew in his gut he had to find Rapture's Edge first if Second Earth was to survive its current state of war. The mythical place had the ability to enhance power to an astronomical level. The one who acquired a vast increase in ability could rule two worlds, which left Duncan and his team with one major goal: *to keep the bad guys on Third from taking possession of Rapture's Edge.*

He glanced at the opposite, semi-opaque grid walls. Images flew by, reflecting the ever-shifting property of the darkening as well as various places on Third Earth. Sometimes deep red flames would appear followed by a stretch of ocean, forest, desert, or cities, then more flames.

The darkening was one of the mysteries of the ascended dimensions, a place 'between', something occurring in each of the five worlds above Mortal Earth.

Third Earth ascenders had built a grid to form a structure through the darkening, making travel through it possible for most ascenders. The fluctuating aspect of this part of nether-space, however, meant he didn't know where he would land if he tried to leave. Though he could blow a hole in the grid wall with his wrecker shotgun, he could easily fall into a wall of fire and be killed instantly.

The darkening required finesse as well as Third Earth power. Neither quality was in his current wheelhouse.

A distant rumbling set another powerful burst of adrenaline plowing his veins. Wreckers.

Rachel, tell Merl to hurry. I've got bad guys on my ass.

Will do.

Remaining in place with his shotgun hidden behind his right leg, he let his preternatural power flow from his wing-locks, up his back, and down his right arm. Once the flow of energy connected with his wrecking shotgun, he could take on a grid wrecker.

A blast from another part of the grid blew a hole in the wall twenty feet distant and brought Duncan face to face with a wrecker. He was a typical Third Earth Militia Warrior, wearing a black leather kilt and maroon battle harness. Three long braids hung on either side of his face.

With a confident smile, he spoke into his com at his shoulder. "I've got him, Your Highness."

Yep, Yolanthe was here.

The wrecker smiled.

Smug asshole.

The split-second the charge flowed over Duncan's weapon, he pivoted, brought his weapon into the open and lifted it to his shoulder.

The wrecker mouthed the words 'oh shit', his brows high as Duncan fired both barrels.

The blast cut the warrior in two and spread his internals over a ten-foot radius. The smell alone was enough to make his stomach curl into a knot.

Plucking two more specialized cartridges from a chest-strap, he reloaded. The sound of additional boots slamming against the grid floor and coming from the same direction as the initial wrecker set his heart into over-drive.

Rachel, he shouted telepathically.

Still here. Merl says he's almost got your location and to get moving.

He turned away from the running feet and while recharging through his wings once more, and gripping his weapon hard, he began to run along the grid in the opposite direction. With any luck, Merl or Rachel would pick up his signal and come to him.

His heart hammered in his ears, the sound like an automatic weapon firing. With his left hand, he wiped sweat from his forehead.

Talk about a nightmare.

I'm on the move, he sent.

I can tell, Rachel returned, each word tense as though she was running right alongside him. *Merl just nodded to me. We've got you on the scanner as well as Yolanthe. She's not far from you. But keep running. Movement helps. We'll fold from our position within fifty yards of your forward trajectory.*

Got it.

Suddenly, Duncan could sense Yolanthe's presence like a wave of heat in front of him. And his wrecking gun wouldn't be able to stop her. The woman had power.

Rachel, she's close now.

We've folded to position and I can hear you running. Keep going. You won't be able to see us because I've got Merl shielded.

Got it.

But Yolanthe materialized, cutting off his path only a dozen feet away from him.

He came to a halt, almost falling into a roll because of his momentum. *Shit. She's right in front of me.*

He tried to fold down the hall, as far as he could see, but Yolanthe lifted a hand and a surge of her power prevented him from moving.

I'm coming to you, Rachel sent, *and I'll use my shield. Merl will hold his current position since he has a location set for Militia Warrior HQ on Two. He's getting ready to blow the grid wall, but our timing will be tight.*

He wanted to respond to Rachel, but Yolanthe had already invaded his mind with her entrancing abilities.

Merl had told Duncan repeatedly he'd need a Third Earth *grayle* power to fend her off. But Duncan hadn't yet been able to access it. For a man supposed to have the power to locate Rapture's Edge, Duncan fell woefully short. He searched within the center of his being for a hint of the *grayle* power, but found nothing.

Instead, he became painfully dizzy as he stared into the woman's pale blue eyes.

Princess Yolanthe had on oddly serene presence as she returned his gaze. "I found you again, Duncan." She held out her arms to him and the dizziness in his head thickened. "Come to me. I've missed you and we have incredible plans to forge together. Come."

She was beautiful in a strange way. A dark purple gloss covered her lips in sickly contrast to her milky white skin. She wore her red hair in at least two dozen thin braids wrapped haphazardly around her head. She looked the same as a month ago when he'd last seen her, wearing a long gown of violet silk to the floor.

Holding his gaze, she added a pressure within his mind, her power beginning to sink deeper and deeper. If she continued, she'd forge another mind-link with him and he'd be lost forever.

"We'll complete our journey together, Duncan. And I'll forgive you everything, I promise."

He began moving toward the woman completely against his will and each of his battle sandals felt weighed down as if covered in cement. The pounding of feet behind him let him know a new squad of wreckers had just arrived, no doubt part of Yolanthe's army, to back her up. He couldn't fight them and he couldn't resist her. If Rachel didn't get to him soon, he was done for.

Yolanthe was ten feet away. Nine … Eight …

With what little strength he had left, he called for help. *Rachel. Trouble.*

Get ready.

He was about to ask, 'For what'. But the next moment he was flying backward and Rachel was on top of him, her protective energy shield vibrating over them both. At the same moment, the deadly trance-like sensations vanished.

"Fire!" He heard Yolanthe shout. She wanted him alive, but if she couldn't have him, she'd kill him to keep him out of the hands of other Third ascenders.

On instinct, Duncan rolled Rachel toward the grid wall as wrecker guns exploded the floor where they'd just been. Holding Rachel tight, he then folded her within the corridor well beyond Yolanthe. And at the exact moment he slipped into nether-space, Yolanthe's wreckers fired into the side walls of the grid. If he hadn't gotten them out of there, they would have both been dead.

Held within Rachel's shield, he gauged the next distance he could take her and landed them down the darkening corridor another thirty feet. Within the grid, he could only fold the distance he could see. If he tried to transport them without seeing a destination, they could end up outside the darkening and anywhere on Third Earth.

He glanced down the corridor. *Where's Merl?*

She smiled, then drew out of his arms. *This way.*

When she took off running, he kept pace. More feet sounded on the grid floor behind them, pounding hard in pursuit. The corridors were curved and branched off at least every twenty yards, a true grid. Rachel kept them moving fast.

Merl's around the next turn. He felt her shift her telepathic communication and knew she was talking to Merl. When her voice returned to him, she said, *He's blasting the grid wall in three ... two ... one.*

The sound of Merl's wrecking gun arrived at the same moment he caught sight of Merl. He felt Rachel's shield disintegrate.

"Good. You're here," Merl shouted. "Move it. We've only got a few seconds."

Duncan reached for Rachel's shoulder and once he made contact, he did a quick fold, taking Rachel to Merl's position. The grid wall wavered as all three of them jumped through the opening.

They landed in the desert at Apache Junction Two, right outside HQ. The rest of the team was there waiting, each of them tense and facing the gaping grid hole, shotguns in hand, all except for Luken.

The leader of the black ops team sat in the dirt at a distance, his face pale, his wings busted.

Duncan jumped to his feet and brought his shotgun to his shoulder. His wing-power still flowed up his back and down his arm, charging his weapon. He listened for the faint rumbling sound of an imminent wrecker assault, but the grid was quiet until finally the shattered wall began to fade then disappear.

It was over.

Even Yolanthe wouldn't be able to find them now because of the constantly shifting nature of nether-space.

He breathed a heavy sigh of relief.

Luken leaned forward slightly as Horace, the most powerful healer on Second Earth, worked on his wings. Luken had attempted a fold in full-mount and when he'd materialized, his wings had been twisted. None of them could do it yet, not even Luken who had the most natural power of any of them.

Luken's lips were a white seam. Still, he called out, "What the hell happened? You were supposed to be on a recon mission to locate a base camp."

Duncan gave a quick rundown of events, ending with, "Yolanthe showed up."

The squad muttered a few obscenities.

"Sounds like she has your signature." Luken shifted his gaze to Merl. "Can she fold someone using a wrist scanner? Is that how she did this?"

Merl shrugged. "Maybe. Although, she might have done the initial fold from the Grid Operating Center. Either way, she has enough power to pull it off."

"If that's the case," Rachel said, "Then why didn't she take Duncan with her when she had the chance?"

Merl shut his scanner down. "It's obvious she has limits and I'll thank the Creator for it."

Luken met Merl's gaze. "Was Duncan taken when he was shielded? Did Yolanthe have the power to remove him while Rachel covered him with her shield?" He glanced at both Duncan and Rachel, then back to Merl.

Rachel lifted her chin. "I wasn't shielding either Merl or Duncan when we went into the grid. I only intended to use the power if wreckers approached. As soon as Duncan was taken, I shielded Merl, but it was never the plan to go in shielded."

"Fuck." Luken pulled his hands into a pair of powerful fists. "All right, I want to go over this point by point. Spare no detail. Let's see if we can figure this out, how to do better for the next mission, though it seems clear we go in shielded from now on."

~ ~ ~

Yolanthe levitated, holding her skirts against her body as she moved past the dead wrecker. She breathed through her mouth since the stench of ruptured intestines filled the darkening grid. It had been a long time since she'd involved herself in a war zone.

She took her time returning to her private portal. Now that she was inside the darkening, she wanted to stay for a few minutes, to enjoy the quiet nether-space region she rarely entered as well as the images moving quickly by like a silent movie.

She couldn't pierce the darkening on her own; she didn't have that kind of power. But the development of the comprehensive grid, with portals, had made travel possible for anyone wealthy enough to pay for access. She'd created a portal to Merl's home just in case she ever needed to pull him out of Second, but to her knowledge he'd never used it.

However, the thought went through her head: *How did Duncan get into the Third grid?*

Was it possible Merl had a connection to Duncan?

She continued levitating forward. She'd been trying for a month now to reacquire the one man who would have sufficient power in the near future to locate Rapture's Edge. For her, nothing was more important than gaining access to the mythical place since it would provide sufficient power to conquer Second Earth. More importantly, she would be able to lay the valuable resource at her father's feet and prove herself worthy in his eyes. Even his three beloved sons had failed to deliver the most significant weapon possible to their father, the noble Chustaffus of Chicago Three.

But she'd lost Duncan again and all because of Rachel, his shield. Once Rachel had covered Duncan in her power, Yolanthe had been unable to either see Duncan or sense him in any other way. She'd also lost him on her wrist scanner.

But how had either of them gotten into the grid?

When she reached her portal, she used the small scanning band on her left wrist and programmed the grid for her villa in Mexico City Three. The moment the portal synced with her home, she simply touched the arched glowing door, the panel opened, and she stepped into her villa living room.

Her snow leopard lifted his head, ears up, then jumped from the *chaise-longue*, padding toward her. He nuzzled her extended palm and she took her time rubbing his ears and scratching his face.

Instead of moving into the room, however, she found her mind stuck on Merl. Until this very moment, she hadn't considered the possibility of her spy being in any way involved with Duncan. She knew of his liaison with Endelle, of his attempts to seduce the leader of Second Earth, but he'd never said a word about Duncan when he'd reported back to her.

To be fair, neither had she. Merl didn't know of her plans to use Duncan to find Rapture's Edge. But had Merl inadvertently heard things because of his interest in Endelle?

By Duncan's presence in the darkening grid, Yolanthe knew Duncan had made plans of his own. But what a Second ascender hoped to accomplish on Third she couldn't imagine.

On the other hand, when she'd been in the Grid Operations Center and had locked onto Duncan, she'd noticed two other entities with him. Her only interest at the time, however, had been to separate Duncan from the others in order to renew her mind-link.

She divined one of the two had been Rachel since Duncan's supposed *breh* had rescued him with her bizarre Fourth Earth shielding power. But who was the other individual and why had all three been in the grid?

Yolanthe now wished she'd taken some time to investigate the others when she'd first come across Duncan's signature. But she'd been so excited to have located him, she'd folded him away then hurried through her own portal to secure him in the darkening.

A chill went through her as though someone treaded on her grave. She actually turned in a circle, wondering if someone was there. But she saw only the rust-and-cream marble pillars of her Mexico City Three home, her extensive sculpted gardens, and the usual guards on duty.

She took a moment and focused inwardly, reaching telepathically for Merl to see if he might know anything about Duncan or his recent activities. Though Merl was in a separate dimension, she had the power to contact him.

How may I serve, Merl sent. At the sound of his deep resonant voice, a tendril of desire worked through her. She'd tried many times to coax Merl into her bed, but the former and very stubborn Warrior of the Blood had refused.

Do you know anything about Duncan Wallace being in the Third Earth grid? I found him there tonight.

Because the telepathic link had been created, she took a moment to explore Merl's emotions. But all that returned, the only thing she'd ever felt from him, was a profound sense of boredom. *Sorry, Your Highness, but I don't know anything about what that asshole is doing or not doing. I don't run in his circles. For some reason, he and his pals don't like me much.*

Merl was too much of a flirt to gain many friendships. *Even through your recent pursuit of Endelle, you didn't come across Duncan or hear mention of his activities?*

Only the breh-hedden *shit. Besides, Wallace was always too caught up in his own drama to pay any attention to me.* She felt him sigh. *Yolanthe, why don't you let me come home? There's nothing here for me on Second and I'm bored out of my skull.*

Merl had become a rather hopeless creature, pursuing only his lusts. He was less than useful to her now, especially since Darian Greaves had been sent to Fourth Earth. Before Greaves's defeat in a battle against Endelle, Merl had provided her with substantial, ongoing reports on Greaves's attacks against the Second Earth government. And for a while, Yolanthe had actually toyed with the idea of offering to serve as Darian's queen once he conquered Second Earth. Alas, the man had failed miserably to fulfill his ambitions.

Now that Greaves was gone, her conversations with Merl had dwindled. But she thought it possible he could make himself useful once more. *I need information about Duncan. I want you to get close to him and use any means you can. Track his movements, and report back.*

When he remained silent, a soft alarm went off in the back of her head. *Do you understand what I'm asking of you?*

You want me to infiltrate and gather information.

She smiled. *You were never stupid. Just remember our little agreement and stay the course. I need this from you.*

I'm at your service, Princess.

For a moment, only a split-second really, she felt something emanate from Merl just before she ended the telepathic communication. Stroking her leopard's head and rubbing his ears, she felt the flavor of the emotion and what came to her was a sense of panic.

Yolanthe gave herself a shake. She had to be mistaken. What did Merl have to be afraid of, except of course for the contents of the last cell in her below-ground prison?

Ah, her prison. One of her favorite places on her estate.

Maybe it was having a discussion with Merl that gave her the idea, but after a moment, she made her way to the round, stone staircase at the east wing of her villa. She descended slowly, her heartrate ramping up. She would need her sex slaves soon because the sight of her prisoners always fed her libido. In seven of her cells were some of the most famous warriors of Third Earth, each a powerhouse in his own right.

The Militia Warrior guards who tended to her prisoners came to attention. They wore the burgundy leather weapons harness of the Third Earth Militia, black leather kilts, and the traditional three long braids on either side of the face. "Your Highness," the men called out in unison, not looking her in the eye as each brought a sword to his chest in salute.

She nodded, then began a slow progress down the line of cells. She had all seven men shackled and pinned to the walls, some facing away from her, others with a full-frontal view she enjoyed immeasurably. These were no ordinary warriors, but Third Earth Warriors of the Blood, captured at the same time she'd sent Merl to Second Earth.

She loved seeing a fighting man naked and stripped of his power. Each was heavily muscled since she required her prisoners to work out on a daily basis. She wasn't completely inhuman; she had her sex slaves service them once a week as long as they continued to build muscle. She would have enjoyed taking the men into her bed, but she was convinced they'd kill her before she even had a chance to spread her legs.

Guards ranged down the somewhat wide hallway at twenty-foot intervals. She ran a tight ship and in the several centuries she'd kept a working jail, she'd never had one escape. The creation of her formidable mist over her property had been her best safeguard since not even the most powerful inmate could fold out of the prison.

When she reached the last cell, she smiled, for the woman looked lovely. She wore a semi-sheer lavender veil covering her head and draping past her shoulders. A number of silver weights in the shape of tear-drops were attached to the hem of the veil, holding the fabric in place.

The covering had two special properties. The first prevented the woman from utilizing her telepathy except with tremendous pain and the other would deliver a death-vapor if she attempted to remove the veil. She wore a fresh linen gown, supplied weekly.

An unusual kind of power vibrated from the woman, something Yolanthe had never quite understood. It was as though she lived on a different plane while her body remained imprisoned in the villa palace.

"Katlynn, my dear, I spoke with your brother today for the first time in ages."

Katlynn turned slowly in her direction. "You talked to Merl?"

"Yes, I did." Yolanthe smiled. "And I can see you've grown hopeful. But I assure you, he has no intention of attempting a rescue. He knows full well any such act on his part would force me to draw a blade across your throat."

~ ~ ~

Duncan had spent the past several minutes detailing for Luken what happened after he'd gotten separated from Merl and Rachel. Luken was still sitting in the dirt, though Horace had brought in two members of his healing squad to help speed up the wing repair process.

Luken scowled as he shifted his gaze to Merl. "What do you have to say?"

Merl ground his teeth and flared his nostrils. "Your men are holding back. If Duncan had been able to access his Third Earth powers, Yolanthe couldn't have trapped him. I can't teach the unteachable."

Merl's words infuriated Duncan. "Maybe it's not the team's fault. Maybe it's your method, manner, and quality of instruction. I mean, a couple of minutes ago you blanked out when Luken asked you a question. Yeah, I'm thinking it's you."

Merl looked like he wanted to say something, then changed his mind. Even so, he got in Duncan's face, his light blue eyes fierce. "Did you even try to use your *grayle* power?"

He glared back at Merl-the-asshole. "Yes, but with no success."

Merl grimaced. "You're not listening to me, Duncan. You have to seize the power here." Merl slapped a hand against the center of his own battle harness, then Duncan's. "You're rock solid as a Warrior of the Blood on Second, but you've got to bump up your game. Otherwise, you'll be dead before we even set foot on Third Earth."

Each foray through the darkening grid had led them to a nest of wreckers and an intense battle, usually involving Rachel's shield to get them safely out. The team hadn't yet succeeded once in finding a safe landing on Third Earth.

Duncan flared his nostrils. "Tell me something I don't know."

Merl narrowed his eyes and a dark red hue suddenly covered his face. "Get in the game," he shouted, not two inches away from Duncan.

"I am in the game." Duncan withheld a long stream of curses that shot through his head.

"Like hell you are."

Duncan's hands shook. He wanted to punch the bastard, but it wouldn't achieve anything especially since Merl was about to go Third Earth warrior on his ass. He could feel the Third ascender revving up.

Merl turned his back to Duncan. The man's wing-locks were pumped and ready to explode into full-mount.

This was not going to be fun.

As Merl mounted his wings, he disappeared into a fold at exactly the same time. Unbelievable. Dematerializing in full-mount was something none of them could do because it did a serious wing-mangle, at least for Second ascenders. Point-of-fact: Luken, sitting on the ground, surrounded by healers.

But where would Merl appear? Behind Duncan? In front of him?

A new flow of adrenaline hit Duncan's bloodstream.

Merl, who'd served as a Warrior of the Blood in his own dimension decades past, as well as a grid wrecker, would hold nothing back short of slicing Duncan in two with his sword.

Duncan moved in a slow circle, trying to prepare, his sword held wide, knees bent. Merl reappeared with his black-and-violet banded wings shimmering at the tips. A drift of *grayle* smoke rose from his body.

"Fuck," Duncan murmured. He lifted his sword as Merl levitated swiftly a few feet into the air then came down on him like lightning.

Duncan barely blocked the strike with his own sword. And with so much Third Earth power behind the blow, Duncan fell to the ground, flat on his back, the tip of Merl's blade pressed into the unprotected notch above Duncan's sternum. A little more pressure would sever his windpipe, a major artery, and his spine. There'd be no coming back.

Merl stared down at him, his wings wafting in the cool night breeze. The desert in late fall wasn't a bad place to be, unless you were on your back with a sword at your throat.

"You haven't had a vision in a month," Merl said quietly, but through gritted teeth. "And you've left your woman twisting in the wind. What the hell is wrong with you? Can't you see the connection? I'll say it again, *get in the game*." The resonance he added hurt Duncan's ears.

Merl levitated with a faint wing-flap, lifting himself backward a few feet to land on the ground. In one smooth motion, he drew in his wings. All those quick, seamless movements were an amazing demonstration of Merl's Third power, showcasing the skills he'd been trying but failing to teach the team.

Duncan sat up but for the moment remained where he was. He hated the arrogant bastard who'd been ordered to train them in Third Earth ways.

Merl folded his sword away. "This team is fucked."

As Duncan rose to his feet, Merl faced the rest of the group. "Which one of you pansy-ass little girls wants to go one-on-one with me? Any of you?"

"I'll go," Rachel called out. And before anyone could stop her, she plucked one of the daggers from her weapons harness and flung it straight at Merl's throat.

But instead of the blade finding home, something the entire team no doubt wanted right now, the Third Earth bastard actually caught the hilt in his hand and threw the blade to the ground. "Anyone else?"

Luken called out, "Merl, back off. We're done for the night. Everyone, hit the showers or the Ops Cave or whatever the hell you want. We'll pick up again tomorrow evening."

When no one moved, he added in a hard voice, "Go."

Merl picked up Rachel's dagger from the dirt and handed it to her.

"Anything I can do to speed up my throw?" she asked.

He shook his head. "Rachel, it's a Third Earth gift. I don't know what Endelle was thinking creating a team of Second ascenders to do battle on Third."

When he moved away, Owen shoulder-blocked him. But Merl did nothing more than offer a glare before moving on.

They were all on edge and pissed.

Rachel didn't have as much of a problem with Merl as the men did. Though to Merl's credit, he no longer tried to flirt with her. Duncan and Merl had fought a few weeks back and Rachel had intervened, covering Duncan with her shield and forcing the fight to stop. He'd been out of his mind with jealousy because Merl had turned all his flirting charm toward Rachel. At least he'd stopped that shit.

Duncan turned toward Rachel, wanting to say something to her, maybe to apologize again. But as usual, his voice shut down. All he could manage was, "Thanks for saving my ass. Again."

She offered a brief nod, but didn't respond. They were hardly speaking these days unless it was a mission-oriented conversation.

He wished she was pissed off about his having broken up with her a month ago, then he could pretend this wasn't all his fault. Instead, she'd been womanly about the whole thing and had given him space, lots of it. No pressure. But because he was caught in the *breh-hedden*, the myth-that-wasn't-a-myth, even her low-key attitude felt like an unbearable weight on his soul.

He wished she'd yell at him. But she never had, even though he'd basically cut her off after he'd promised 'to try'.

As he watched Rachel fold a cloth into her hand and wipe down the blade, desire for her rose as it always did, like a hurricane within his body. She was his woman, his *breh*, the one destined to bond with him. And he craved her. Even though they'd dated off-and-on for decades, what he felt for her now was beyond description, an ache in his groin, his soul, a profound vibration through his sliced up heart.

She turned toward him. Her lips parted and he understood why. The *breh-hedden* had added a pair of inciting scents to the picture the moment sexual desire rose. No doubt, she smelled his need, which she'd said reminded her of spicy ale.

"Duncan," she said softly, a plea in her voice.

But he couldn't act on what he felt. He'd tried to tell her what was wrong, but he found it impossible to explain why being close to her cut him up inside. He'd called it a snake that bites.

Despite his almost painful craving for her, he turned on his heel and headed toward the entrance to Militia Warrior HQ. He wondered what

Merl had meant when he suggested his disconnect from Rachel was part of his issue in not being able to harness his *grayle* power.

Was it possible Rachel was the key to opening up his Third Earth abilities?

~ ~ ~

Rachel watched Duncan go, her gaze fixed for a long moment on his broad shoulders, then moving down the beautiful line of his back. Duncan had a perfect physique with a lean waist and a firm warrior's ass. The sexy, black leather kilt gave her all kinds of ideas. When she'd caught his spicy ale scent, she'd almost thrown herself at him. She needed him badly and still didn't really understand why he'd cut her off.

She knew he was in pain, enduring a kind of torment she might never fully understand. His father had been a cruel man and his mother had disappeared when he was six. She'd come to believe the combination of both circumstances had poisoned her man. It was possible he'd never come back to her despite the pull of the *breh-hedden*.

Meanwhile, she kept her tears to herself.

She finished cleaning off her dagger then slid it into her battle-harness.

Luken called to her. "You did good tonight, Rachel. Thanks for stepping up."

She waved in his direction, but she was too tired to offer more than a half-smile. She thought Luken was one of the finest men she'd ever known, much in Duncan's mold. The problem was Duncan didn't believe he was worth a damn. Maybe that was why she had tremendous grace for him right now. And she loved him. He was her man, her *breh*.

She rotated her throwing arm slowly then pulled her elbow with her opposing hand to stretch a few of her nagging back muscles. She was exhausted, as usual, from the night's work, and really sore in a variety of places. It was a testament to a month's training that she no longer lost her cookies at the sight of blood or blown-up wreckers. For the past month the team had either battled death vampires at the Second Earth Borderlands as part of their training, or faced off with wreckers in the Third Earth darkening grid.

And of course, since Yolanthe now had a bead on Duncan, the game had taken a brand new terrifying turn.

She was learning a lot, but progress was way too slow. The entire team lived with a constant sense of urgency, a collective need to be heading to Third. From the beginning, Endelle's vision had made it clear the fate of two worlds depended on the black ops team getting to Third and doing some good, especially Duncan and Luken.

Luken was worried, though he hid it well. Merl was right. How could a team of Second ascenders hope to do battle against the most powerful forces on Third Earth? The disparity in preternatural power alone made the situation untenable. But none of the men were quitters and each would die doing all they could to make the team work.

She was no different. Once having committed to becoming a warrior, she was all in.

She headed to the bathroom and did a superficial clean-up, removing as much of the blood spatter as she could. She didn't like to shower at HQ, but she wasn't exactly ready to head home either.

Her black leather flight suit and weapons harness would have to be laundered. She had twelve battle suits in all and now understood why Luken had insisted so many were necessary.

Every night ended in some kind of damage to her uniform and so sweat-stained both laundering and mending were needed by the time dawn rolled around.

Besides, she had an itch and she was hoping against hope maybe she could talk Duncan into sharing her bed tonight. She'd caught his scent. He wasn't indifferent to her. Maybe she could seduce him, despite his troubled spirit.

Well, a woman could dream.

Chapter Two

Change comes,
Not when the spirit grows willing,
But when the battle has exhausted the flesh.
Collected Proverbs — **Beatrice of Fourth**

Endelle sat on the side of her *chaise-longue* in her secret, India Two home. Her tigers roared at her monkeys, who in turn kept screeching their replies.

She held a sketch pad in hand with several pieces of chalk in a container next to her. Spread out around her feet were a dozen drawings. She'd always loved designing her clothes, one of the activities of her 9000 years of vampire service, which, like good sex, had helped keep her sane.

She wasn't an artist, not being able to truly translate all she saw in her head onto paper. But she'd gotten good enough over the years to render sufficiently detailed drawings for her head seamstress to interpret her concepts with ease. The talented woman had a crew of ten at her beck-and-call and could execute even the most complicated outfit in a matter of hours.

As her gaze roved the scattered drawings on the floor, her eyes suddenly popped wide. She felt as though she'd been caught in some kind of trance because until this moment, she hadn't recognized the obvious theme.

But there it was with swords, intricately carved wood shields, metal headdresses with horns, tough thigh boots, and spikes on leather wrist guards. One short skirt was made of chain-mail, another of black leather, and a third of crimson silk embroidered with gold daggers.

Seems she had war on her mind.

Setting her chalk and her sketchpad aside, she rubbed her forehead with the tips of her fingers. She'd been feeling a tremendous pressure lately, wishing it would go away. Not a headache, exactly, but a weight within her mind. Yet no amount of self-healing would relieve the sensation.

Earlier, she'd met her favorite prostitute at the door, only to hand him his usual fee, wipe his mind clean, then send him away without having taken him to bed. Though she was desperate for release, she knew the man's usual oral gifts weren't going to get the job done.

She rose from her seat and moved into the stone-paved courtyard. The air was humid and heavy, just like her spirits. A tiger rubbed his head against her hip, and she took a moment to scratch his face with her fingernails. The beast chuffed at her in gratitude then flopped down at her feet.

But she kept moving.

She had her routine: massages as often as needed, lots of government meetings she detested, and a once-a-week workout with her favorite for-hire boy-toy here in India.

The long courtyard had a large rectangular pond and in the center an island housing a mature Indian laurel. Lily-pads dotted the dark green lake and the monkeys raced from the branches of the tree to the tall, two-story roofline and back.

Usually, she could figure out exactly what was bugging her without having to blink twice, but her current mood had her flummoxed. And she'd rather have ants chewing on her butt than spend even a second analyzing her innermost psyche.

What held her attention the most was the fucked up vision she'd had about Luken and his not-so-bright future on Third Earth. She'd ordered him to pull a black ops team together to handle forays into Third Earth and some of the results had been nothing short of spectacular. Three Militia Warriors and one peace-loving female had risen in the space of a single, astonishing month to Warrior of the Blood level.

Unheard of.

During the celebration, however, Merl had killed her feel-good.

Standing beside her at the induction ceremony, he'd muttered, "Much good any of this will do us on Third. Your team might as well be throwing dead fish and hoping they somehow turn into grenades."

She'd almost jumped down his throat, but dammit the bastard was right.

The black ops team wasn't anywhere near ready to battle the powerful Militia Warriors and death vampires they'd be confronting on Third.

What the hell had she been thinking trying to create a black ops team out of Second ascenders? Except she'd seen both Duncan and Luken battling on Third Earth and she'd felt compelled to act. She also knew from the vision both Second and Third Earth were on the brink of total domination by a psychopath even more formidable than her former adversary, Darian Greaves. Even thinking about Chustaffus and the slave world he'd built on Third sent icy chills down her spine.

Damn that vision to all thirteen layers of hell. And the day she decided a series of most-excellent orgasms wouldn't fix her up, was the day she knew she was in some deep, stinky shit.

Only where exactly was a woman of her stature and power supposed to find answers? If *she* didn't know what to do, who would?

As she moved along the stone path around the perimeter of the pond, her thoughts turned once more to Luken. She pressed a hand to her breastbone, her throat tight. An ache had formed in the middle of her chest like a stone and seemed to grow bigger each time she thought about the blond, god-like warrior.

He'd always been the peacekeeper among the Warriors of the Blood and a favorite of hers, when he'd served under Thorne and later as the leader of the team. Of course, this was in times past, before the *breh-hedden* had picked off several of her elite troops. With a woman to love, each man had morphed into something new, with greater powers and a bigger role in her government.

Luken hadn't yet been so fortunate. He was still very much a bachelor. And worse, the only vision Endelle had ever had suggested Luken's time was up.

For a month now, the vision burned in her head with a creeping, constant fame. Luken had been high in the air, battling death vampires, and one of them had sent his blade through Luken's spine. She'd watched him fall through the sky, presumably to his death.

But what had the vision really meant?

The added, constant pressure in her head made her wonder if maybe she was meant to do more than just assemble a black ops team? Was some ascended element working on her, trying to move her down a different path?

She wasn't a woman of great faith, not after having lived such a long time and seen what murderous intent most humans were capable of no matter what dimension. If anything, she imagined the Creator walking around, gripping his hands, shaking his head, wondering what the hell he'd been thinking to pull man out of the mud in the first place.

Maybe she didn't have answers to her questions, but her instincts warned her some kind of action was necessary. She couldn't let Luken go to his death on Third without putting up a fight.

As she made her way back to her *chaise-longue* and all the warrior costumes she'd sketched, she still had no idea what the hell she should do. Except of course, she'd definitely get her staff going on a few of these sketches. The more she looked at them, the more her heart settled down.

She might as well have some fun while she watched two worlds go to hell.

~ ~ ~

Rachel sat on a stool at the bar in the Ops Cave, arms aching, thigh muscles on fire. She was edgy as well, but not from either the nightly drills, battling death vampires, or the recent escape from Yolanthe's clutches.

Instead, her libido was wearing on her. Maybe it was a warrior thing, but she needed to be on her back and Duncan doing what he did best. However, the man was barely speaking to her unless it related to the business of making war.

And no arguments on her part had changed a damn thing.

She sipped a glass of water. The men drank harder stuff, but her stomach was too unsettled to chance it. Nausea had accompanied her battle training. And why wouldn't it? No one should have to see such a large amount of blood and other kinds of human debris, night-after-night.

The first time she'd seen a Third Earth wrecker killed, she'd thrown up the contents of her stomach, then continued on with a long bout of the dry heaves. Same thing had happened when one of her daggers had found the throat of a 'pretty boy' for the first time. The beautiful death vampire had fallen over, and she'd watched the life drain out of him.

Though she didn't wield a sword like the men, she practiced throwing her daggers two hours every night. More than once, she'd saved one of her team a lot of hurt by intervening with a sharp blade.

For the first week, she didn't understand how the men faced the battlefield night after night. A month later, she'd built an iron wall around her initial sensitivity and horror. She no longer had nightmares either, but slept like a baby.

Duncan had helped. He'd reminded her in detail how death vampires were addicted to a powerful substance which could only be reached at the point of death. Once enslaved to dying blood, getting the next fix was all the pretty boys thought about. They were in most respects similar to the vampire lore of Mortal Earth, with pale, almost bluish skin and mesmerizing beauty.

By her third week of training and battling, she'd come to celebrate each death along with the men, knowing how many lives she and her team had saved.

Her purpose in the field also included learning how to shield all the warriors, not just Duncan. Because even the lowliest Militia Warrior on Third would outmatch the most powerful Warrior of the Blood on Second, her ability to shield the team had become her most significant contribution.

The trouble was, the whole team pretty much sucked in terms of having the chops to battle on Third Earth. So how the hell were they supposed to go to Third and save the world?

With dawn closing in, the team now lounged in their hang-out at Militia Warrior HQ. Luken had commandeered the large rec room specifically for the team.

By quickly acquired ritual, they were all here or in the immediate vicinity. The bathrooms and locker rooms were nearby and the men often made phone calls arranging hookups or any other point of business after a night of fighting. Or sometimes one of their number ordered pizza and wings and they'd dig in as a team.

She'd passed Duncan on the way in, but he hadn't even made eye contact with her. Typical. He'd been talking to good-natured Alex, probably comparing notes on how much they each despised Merl.

At least he was talking to someone.

She leaned an elbow on the bar, then lifted her ponytail. She was still hot and sweaty, grateful the Ops Cave had the air-conditioner blasting. She wasn't sure why, but her breasts hurt something fierce. Maybe her weapons harness needed another adjustment.

She flipped the side tab, which let out the seam a little on the thick metal-and-leather garment. She almost groaned with relief. She switched to the other side and repeated. Better. Much better. She'd have to remove the harness in order to do a full adjustment involving the side straps and locking mechanism, but for now, she wasn't in quite as much discomfort.

But what was with her breasts? Was this another result of the freaking *breh-hedden* that besides craving sex with her man, her breasts had gotten bigger? Forget implants, just get struck down by vampire mate-bonding and snap, bigger boobs.

Yeah, she was tired.

She sipped some more. The cool glass against her lips felt like heaven as well. She was tired and she wanted her bed. Yet, more than her bed, she wanted a man. She wanted Duncan.

Her gaze took a slow drift around the room. Duncan still hadn't come in, but what a collection of muscle.

And here was the other side of the equation. It did not help her overwrought libido to be surrounded by so much masculine gorgeousness. Whatever else the black ops team might be, these men rocked.

Owen sat next to the pool table, a beer in his left hand while with his right he made a fist and flexed his bicep. He had a healthy bruise across the top and was probably performing a bit of self-healing. The sight of the bulge, however, accompanied by a sexy flex-and-release put a hitch in her breathing.

Owen was an intense warrior and ridiculously handsome. He had a cleft chin, brown hair with natural golden highlights, and hazel eyes. A sexy three-inch scar ran at an angle below his left cheekbone, acquired before he ascended. Over the last month, since the team had formed, she'd watched women touch him there, knowing full-well they'd be touching something else later.

What was it about a scar on a man?

Merl didn't have any scars, at least none she knew of, though she had glimpsed a tattoo etched down the center of his back. He was a powerful Third ascender and sat in a corner apart, a hard expression on his face. Gone were his flirtations from a month ago and he no longer stuck close to Endelle. In many ways, he seemed like a different man altogether.

He held a cigarette in one hand and with his other rubbed the stem of a martini glass. He'd switched up his more recent Grey Goose martinis for a sweeter French version, with pineapple juice and blackberry liqueur.

Merl with his light blue eyes was fiercely independent, a man unto himself. He didn't give a damn what any of the other warriors thought of him. He looked rugged to Rachel in a way that made her certain he'd lived for centuries and not just decades.

She'd tried talking to him a few days ago, but he'd clammed up, shifting his gaze purposefully to Duncan. She'd gotten the message. Merl might not be one of her favorite people, but he worked hard now to respect Duncan's claim on her, such as it was.

Damn *breh-hedden*. Duncan had become as distant as the faintest star and about as warm.

"Rachel," Joshua called to her. "I gotta ask. Do you remember a time when you *weren't* a warrior?"

Joshua, brown eyes glittering, had settled into the couch, stretching out his long legs. He shifted to sit low so his head would hit the back. He was as badass as they came, with thick, dark brown hair and bulked up shoulders. He had the look of a hunter, his gaze constantly searching whatever space he happened to be in. He'd removed his leather wrist-guards, putting his tattoos on display. Black flames, morphing into birds in flight, began at the wrist and rose almost to his elbows.

His shin-guards were gone as well and because all the men battled in black leather kilts, she had a view of muscular and very shapely legs. She'd never thought of men's legs as 'shapely', not until this moment.

But boy could she imagine her hands gliding along the tight muscular curve that ran all the way to the ankle.

As this completely inappropriate and very heated thought blasted through her head, she looked away. Ignoring her errant thoughts, she answered his question. "All I can say is tonight I feel like I've been making war for centuries." The men chuckled.

She sipped her water again, hoping it would cool her down.

"Well," Josh added, "You're doing great."

"Thanks."

She'd changed so much in the past month. For decades, from the time she'd escaped her abusive, now-deceased ex-husband, she'd pursued a peaceful organic life. But in the course of the last few weeks, she'd arrived at a rare level of power for a woman in the ascended world: she'd become a Warrior of the Blood.

They all had, joining Luken and Duncan, though Merl eclipsed them all as a Third Earth What-Bee.

She'd laughed the first time she'd heard the slang term for Warrior of the Blood. The Militia Warriors, being mostly men, never offered a compliment when they could deliver a jab. So, 'What-Bees' it was.

But four of the warriors rising in the ranks so swiftly had the entire Militia Warrior community hyped up with all sorts of expectations.

Sweet Jesus, how her life had changed.

Alex strolled in, his steely gray eyes narrowed. He rubbed the wrinkled skin of his scarred shoulder, the one burned before he entered his rite of ascension. Though lean, he had muscle on muscle and moved with a swagger as though pushing the air aside to make way for his awesomeness.

And he was awesome. Alex tended to lift a room rather than bring it down. Though he was as tough as the rest of the warriors, his glass was always half full.

Luken followed a minute later, a deep pit between his brows, his clear blue eyes tightened with concern. He'd removed his *cadroen* and his long blond hair hung around his weighty shoulders. The leader of the squad did not look happy, but then the fold he'd attempted had torn up the mesh super-structure which held the wings together.

He was all healed up, but his face was still pale. Busted wings *hurt*.

He looked around, his gaze landing on her for a moment, before he asked, "Where's Duncan?"

"He was in the hall talking to Alex. And since Alex is already here, I don't know where Duncan is. On the phone, maybe." She shrugged.

Duncan had been so remote of late, even Luken didn't evince the smallest surprise at her answer. The entire team knew they'd split up, though she currently resided in his home.

No one knew what to do with Duncan, not even Luken who could usually draw a bead on one of his team's issues, then work swiftly to get the problem resolved. But he'd become increasingly distant with everyone.

Though his visions had been his strongest emerging power, he hadn't had a single one since the recent battle at Endelle's palace. For months, prior to Yolanthe entrancing him, he'd utilized his visions during battle in order to lay out the position of the enemy and in doing so, he'd saved a lot of lives. As Merl had indicated earlier outside, his visions had all but dried up.

Luken moved in the direction of the bar, sliding behind to slam a tumbler on the counter and pour a scotch, neat. He threw it back and poured another.

Her lips twisted. "Well, you sure had some fun tonight."

He met her gaze. Damn, but Luken had the most beautiful blue eyes, as clear as a Caribbean sea. His hair was almost as blond as hers and even longer.

"How you doin', Rachel? You've become one helluva a fighter in the past month. You look born to it out there, like your brother Gideon. Sure you don't want to take up sword-work?"

She shook her head. "I can hardly lift the practice sword you gave me. I don't have the muscle."

He settled his elbows on the bar and sipped his scotch. Of course, with his back hunched, his shoulders appeared extra-massive, sending shivers over her arms and down her sides.

She swiveled slowly away from him, her skin on fire as desire rippled through her. Creator help her, she couldn't start lusting after Luken.

He patted her arm and it was all she could do to keep from moaning. She felt guilty as hell, but she was a man-hungry, hormonal mess. The *breh-hedden* had crashed down on her and now all she could think about was sex, Duncan's hot-as-hell body, and how she wasn't gettin' any.

"Rachel? What the fuck?" Duncan's deep voice hit the air.

She pivoted slightly, swiveling once more on her stool, as she turned in the direction of the entrance. Duncan stood in the doorway, scowling at her.

Oh, shit. Busted. But maybe it wasn't a bad thing. Duncan ought to get a clear picture of the state she was in.

For a moment, time slowed to a standstill and all she saw was his thick, dark brown hair, in waves to his shoulders and his beautiful green eyes. He began moving toward her, walking with his usual lethal grace, the way a stallion would move, muscles quivering.

His eyes always got to her, an incredible green, heavily fringed with black lashes. His dark brows were thick and arched. His symmetrical features gave him a powerful appearance with high, pronounced cheekbones and a strong, angled jaw.

His nostrils flared. Her scent had to be flooding the room given the level of her need.

He crossed quickly to her and at the same time, Luken moved almost as fast to get out of Duncan's way.

When Duncan got close enough, she slid from the stool to stand

31

about a half inch away from him and gripped both sides of his weapons harness. "We need to talk." Her voice sounded hoarse.

His green eyes flashed, but he addressed her telepathically, *What I want to know is why the hell your garden scent has suddenly filled this space?*

She glared in response. *Why do you think?*

He took her arm and guided her none too gently toward the hall. "Fine. Then let's talk."

Once in the hall, he continued on, moving her at least thirty feet away from the Ops Cave door and spoke in a hushed voice. "Were you thinking about taking up with one of my men? Is that what's going on? You like Josh's tats? Owen's scar?" Owen, Josh, and Alex had been part of Duncan's Militia Warrior squad before they became part of the black ops team.

She lifted her chin. "What do you expect? I have needs, and you've made it clear you don't want any part of me." He still held her left arm in a tight grip, and because she wanted the contact, she didn't pull away. Instead, she stroked his battle vest, rubbing her fingers over the stiff, black leather, aiming for the edge so she could slip onto some skin.

When she found flesh, Duncan's spicy ale scent sharpened. She took it as a good sign and caressed his shoulder. His lips parted and his breathing grew rough. No surprise there. She knew Duncan wanted her; he just didn't seem to have permission to be with her.

"What are you doing?" he asked.

"You know exactly what I'm doing."

"You need to stop." He caught her hand and pulled it away from his shoulder. "I can't do this shit right now."

She lifted her gaze to his. He frowned, so she frowned back. "Why not? You won't talk to me, you won't tell me a damn thing and I need you, Duncan, your body pressed up against me and none of this leather between us. Just skin. Yours and mine. And something hard driving between my legs."

He closed his eyes and waves of his scent flowed. She was more hopeful than she'd been in the past four weeks.

"Duncan, try not to think of *us* right now. Think of this as a one-night-stand, only with me." How desperate was she to be begging, but she didn't care. "Just take me to bed tonight. I need you. I can't explain why, but I'm going crazy."

Finally, he released her arm and stepped away from her. "I've said all I'm going to say."

"Then who's going to take care of me?"

He winced, but he turned up the hall. "I'm heading home. You coming?"

"No."

"Suit yourself."

She watched him go, walking up the long hall, heading toward the landing platforms. The only way to leave Militia HQ was via the platforms or the alarms would go off.

"Why won't you talk to me?" she called after him, shouting at his back. "Dammit, Duncan! You said you would try. You promised me you would try."

But he didn't respond.

He'd told her he couldn't take it anymore. A snake lived inside him, filling him with poison, and he didn't want to hurt her.

But he'd hurt her anyway, idiot that he was.

And he wouldn't talk to her.

She sighed heavily as she returned to the Ops Cave, not wanting to follow Duncan just yet. She lived in the master bedroom of his Paradise Valley Two home, while Duncan had moved to a guest room. He'd insisted she stay since her beautiful forest cottage had been destroyed by Third Earth wreckers. Duncan's offer of shelter made him a good man, which hurt her all the more.

She took up her bar stool once more, and continued sipping her water. She was queasy, probably because of fatigue and a too-tight weapons harness. She rubbed the dagger hilts of the two blades angled along her waist.

None of the men would meet her gaze. Each stared at the floor or the walls, anything but her.

She felt like apologizing for making a scene. But she knew these guys; they'd only be embarrassed. They'd probably heard most of the exchange anyway, vampire hearing being as sensitive as it was. And most certainly, they'd heard her shouting at Duncan. But they were a team now, and very little could remain hidden, especially when it came to a relationship between two members. Besides, they ought to have an understanding of what was going on between herself and Duncan.

She just wished to hell she knew what to do with him.

Chapter Three

Sometimes surrender requires
The greatest courage of all.
Collected Proverbs – **Beatrice of Fourth**

Duncan reached the out-going landing platform, got the okay from the Militia Warrior in charge, and folded himself straight to his bathroom at his Paradise Valley home.

His thighs tingled up through his groin and all because the *breh-hedden* kept torturing him with Rachel's rich garden scent. He sniffed his shoulder near his weapons harness. Rachel had touched him there, fondling his muscles. He could still smell her on him and he wanted more, craved more.

He was in pain.

Sure, he took care of himself in the shower, and always with images of Rachel streaming through his head. But it wasn't the same as being buried deep, tasting her blood on his lips, hearing her moan. He loved the sounds she made when she was aroused and especially when she came.

Tonight, he'd almost relented. Even now, he listened hard to any sound of Rachel returning home, wondering if he should go to her.

He'd given her the master bedroom for the duration. A month ago, wreckers had taken her cottage down to the foundation in the Seattle One Colony. Yolanthe had wanted Rachel dead for the simple reason Rachel had the power to create a protective shield around him, something she'd done tonight.

In the meantime, Rachel had nowhere else to go so of course he'd offered his home, even if he couldn't be close. He'd thought about moving into his cabin on the Mogollon Rim, a place he'd bought several months ago, but he didn't feel easy about being separated from her. If Yolanthe ever located Rachel on her own, the madwoman would kill her.

He stripped off his battle leathers and put them in a hamper. His housekeeper came by every afternoon, picked up whatever was there, then took it to Murphy's for laundering. He had good staff.

He punched his chest with his fist a couple of times, wishing he could fix what was wrong inside him. He hated himself for not being with Rachel, for not taking care of her. But proximity had become a snake that bit hard, adding poison until his gut writhed and he could hardly breathe.

Stepping into the shower, he moved under a hot stream of water and worked at letting go. He scrubbed his body down hard, washed his hair, tried to relax. But a half hour later, after toweling dry, he still felt like shit and knew sleep wouldn't find him anytime soon.

He put on some shorts and headed to his workout room. After a few minutes of stretching, then jogging on his treadmill to warm up, he gave himself to a whole lot of iron and a punishing regimen.

Though he'd spent hours battling death vampires, grid wreckers, and trying but failing to reach some level of competence with Merl's Third Earth drills, he still wasn't loose.

A good lay would have helped. For that reason alone, he'd almost taken Rachel up on her offer.

Rachel.

God help him.

Ten lifts. Switch up the weights. Ten more. Repeat.

He was sweating hard.

Moving to the leg curl bench, he worked out his quads. Every few minutes, he'd switch to another station, and hammer a different set of muscles.

A half hour passed, then an hour. Dawn had come and gone.

When Rachel finally came home, he heard her call to him, letting him know she'd arrived safely.

"Good," he responded.

Brilliant of him.

He squeezed his eyes shut and tried to keep a lid on how much he craved her right now.

He recalled how she'd been lusting after the other men and his *brehhedden* reflexes suddenly vaulted into another searing overdrive. He took several deep breaths, struggling to get calm. He even growled and his fangs made an appearance. Still, he remained where he was and put his weights in motion again.

How could he explain to Rachel what his life was like, what it had always been? A viper lived inside him and had from the time he could remember, a serpent moving through thick waters, writhing and biting when he got too close to anyone. He'd promised himself long ago to keep his distance from any serious relationship.

He'd made an exception with Rachel repeatedly over the decades, but he'd always found a way to end things, usually forcing her to break up with him.

He had nothing to give, not a damn thing.

Now that she was home, her scent, like earth and flowers, the smell of grass in springtime, of life and growing things, wafted into his workout room. He wanted her so bad he ached for her, ached to have his cock buried deep between her legs, his body moving over hers, his arms surrounding her, his fangs in her neck, her earthy blood flowing down his throat. And he wanted her tasting him, feeding from him, taking him inside her body, her mouth, her well.

Rachel. How he loved her.

The snake swirled faster now, jaws unhinged, sharp fangs dripping with poison.

He left the weights and hopped onto the rowing machine. He set a heavy pace, one intended to squeeze every ounce of water from his body.

But the snake moved faster and he knew this would be a bad one.

The memory rose sharp and clear of his mother's arms around him, her tears wet on his young six-year-old neck. "You'll be safer without me here," she had said. "You have to understand, Duncan. You'll be safe, but only if I leave."

The serpent's fangs bit deep.

He stopped rowing and roared the pain of the bite, of watching his mother walk through the front door to never come back, of falling into his father's rigid discipline as he stood in one place for hours, as his father hit him to make him stronger, cut him, whipped him.

He rolled off the machine and fell onto the floor, shaking. The poison was in his veins now and wouldn't come out.

He had nothing to give Rachel.

Nothing.

~ ~ ~

Rachel sat up in bed. Duncan's anguished shouts had awakened her, pounding against her chest and forcing tears to her eyes. He'd been doing this a lot lately, roaring when he spent a couple of hours in his gym. The sound of his suffering had helped her to understand the level of pain he was in.

She'd tried more than once to encourage him to tell her what was going on, but her presence only seemed to add to his suffering.

She rubbed her temples and prayed for wisdom, something beyond herself to help the man she loved.

After a moment, her spirit grew quiet and in its place was a small sense of peace and the soft words floating though her mind, *He'll figure this out. You'll see.*

She lay back down in bed. Her nausea was better but her current man-hungry state wouldn't let her fall back to sleep. Her craving for Duncan had returned, stronger than ever. She didn't know what to do. She'd tried pleasuring herself, but for whatever reason, it didn't help at all. Instead, her thoughts became fixed on the last time they'd made love in this bed, how Duncan had sucked on her wing-locks and made her come.

She groaned, put a pillow over her head, and screamed her frustration.

~ ~ ~

For the past two hours, Luken had watched Merl closely, waiting him out. The brother had smoked cig after cig and downed at least three martinis. He stared off into space, his gaze fixed on nothing in particular. He'd been attached to Endelle for weeks, playing her court jester. But the moment the black ops team had come together, he'd abandoned the Supreme High Administrator of Second Earth.

Since then, however, Merl had turned into a morose, distant warrior, hostile at times. He even seemed despondent, though Luken wasn't sure exactly why. Merl was supposed to bring the team up to Third Earth battle levels. But so far none of them could properly execute the drills, especially the retrieval of *grayle* power, a Third specialty.

Merl badgered the team constantly about how each one of them was holding back. But what about Merl? Though he outdistanced each of them in power, he was completely shut down.

Luken's instincts told him he didn't have a full picture yet of Merl, in particular, what was bugging the shit out of him. And tonight, Luken intended to get some answers. He wasn't about to leave the Ops Cave until he'd had words with the Third ascender.

He sipped his fifth Scotch, enjoying the muscle-easing buzz while sitting in a leather chair near the door. He had his long, heavy legs balanced on a sturdy ottoman.

In terms of Second Earth, the team had taken huge strides. Each of the three Militia Warriors had made the leap to Warrior of the Blood. The average Militia Warrior had to work as part of a team of four in order to bring down a single Second Earth death vampire. A Warrior of the Blood, on the other hand, could destroy several at a time on his own.

Even Rachel now had What-Bee battle abilities. She'd been the biggest surprise of all. The woman who had proclaimed peace for decades, had finally accepted her fighting mantle. She had remarkable power levels and possessed a fighting spirit much like her brother, Gideon.

She didn't use a sword, not possessing the physical strength to wield the heavy blades. But she'd rapidly perfected her dagger skills and had taken out her fair share of pretty-boys. One month in, she'd developed a tough warrior skin, seeing the enemy for the addicted monsters they'd become.

Luken had been worried sick about her at first and her initial reactions to the usual gore of battle had been completely predictable. She'd come through, however, with tremendous strength and a kind of centered poise not often seen in novice warriors. He was damn impressed with her.

Merl rose to his feet and finally met Luken's gaze. "Thought you'd be tucked in bed by now." The cigarette in his hand disappeared. Merl had a trick of folding them away as well as his martini glasses. Presumably his smoking and drinking detritus ended up back at his house.

Luken didn't flinch. "I've been getting my kicks watching you pout instead."

Merl scowled and each nostril flared. "And how did you like doing your fold tonight? Bet that felt like floating on clouds."

Luken repressed a shudder; his mangled wings had hurt like a bitch. He stood up, offering a casual shrug. "Thought I had it. Guess I was wrong."

"Guess you were." Merl moved slowly, like a man used to meeting up with thugs in an alley. He was as muscled as Duncan and clearly put in long hours pumping iron like the rest of them, but he was always looking over his shoulder.

He was a handsome bastard, with light blue eyes and strong features made more pronounced by the way he combed his hair straight back. He refused to grow it out warrior long, the only member of the team who wasn't following protocol. But then Merl had been exiled while serving as a What-Bee on Third. Maybe he'd gotten burned and no longer valued the traditions. The truth was, no one knew much about Merl; he wasn't talking to any of them.

Luken tried a different tack. "I need you to tell me something."

"Not gonna spill my guts."

Luken took his measure. "Not asking you to. I just want a straight up answer to a single question. Can you give me that?"

"Ask me and we'll see."

The man was dug in.

"Why did you quit the palace? You and Endelle were like a matched pair of socks. Then suddenly you dumped her."

For some reason, Merl didn't seem bothered by the subject, which told Luken he'd missed what was really distressing Merl by about a mile.

He pushed his fingers through his hair. "I get Endelle and she gets me. She had no expectations and neither did I. I also hadn't planned on being assigned to a black ops team, but I'm here now and I'm taking my job seriously. Call it pouting if you want, but your team isn't anywhere near ready to battle Third Earth death vampires or even Militia Warriors in any dimension above Second. Yet I can sense we'll be moving out soon, which basically is a death sentence. Is that enough of an answer?"

Luken could only frown in response.

Merl grimaced. "That's what I thought." He headed toward the door and Luken didn't try to stop him.

Merl was a complicated man. The most Luken really knew was both sides of the conflict on Third had wanted Merl dead. He'd been exiled to Second Earth where he'd lived for fifty years.

What Luken really couldn't figure out, however, was how to get the team up to a basic Third battling level. And like Merl, every instinct told Luken their time was almost up.

~ ~ ~

Duncan lay on the floor of his workout room, staring up at the vaulted ceiling. The memory of his mother leaving had come back like a train that jumped the rails and kept throwing cars off the tracks.

When he sat up, he rocked, trying to dispel the pain engulfing him.

His father, Carlyon, had never shown him photos of his mother so he'd never had any kind of image of her in his head. And even though he could recall her voice as she clung to him, and watch her back as she left, he still didn't know what she looked like.

His father hadn't helped, of course. Carlyon had expressed his hatred of her hundreds of times. He'd made it clear repeatedly that Duncan had been abandoned because his mother had never loved him, never wanted him.

But he wasn't a child any longer as he considered the memory. He was a grown man, one who had come to despise Carlyon for the brute he was.

As he lay on the floor, he reviewed her words again: *You have to understand, Duncan. You'll be safe, but only if I leave.*

Was it possible she hadn't wanted to leave? Until this moment, he'd never considered anything other than what Carlyon had told him.

He couldn't pretend to understand what it was like for a woman who'd been abused and beaten by her husband, the man who'd sworn to love and protect her. But Rachel had shared many details about her experience as Grieg's wife, and how abusive men often applied a process of terror and guilt, threatening not just the woman's life but the lives of those she loved as well.

Carlyon wouldn't have hesitated to use Duncan in his battle to control Duncan's mother.

He finally rose to his feet, his mind caught in the past and focused on the night his mother had left him in the hands of a monster. Would Carlyon have killed them both if his mother had stayed?

He headed back to the shower, and once more let the heat of the water work some kind of ease into his body. Afterward, he donned pajama bottoms and sat outside on the back patio in the early morning light. Paradise Lake was beautiful with sunlight glittering on the water.

He drank a sports drink to replenish his fluids. He needed his bed, but he damn well knew sleep wouldn't come, not this morning.

His thoughts slipped back to just before dawn when he'd caught Rachel lusting after her teammates. Her scent had reached him well down the hallway, when he'd finally decided to make an appearance at the Ops Cave. Her mating scent, thick with pheromones only he could perceive, had sent desire trailing down his abdomen into his groin.

He'd taken in the picture immediately. Rachel was staring at Owen's flexed arm. The rest of the men, built like all hell, had no doubt worked for her like a club full of male strippers.

He knew women had needs and the *breh-hedden* had sent hers into overdrive, just like his. He'd reacted like a caveman, all but dragging her into the hall and calling her out because her garden scent had told its own tale. But what right did he have to condemn her when he refused to take care of her himself?

None.

Rachel.

Oh, God, Rachel.

He'd wanted her badly. She'd looked beautiful with her skin flushed and her blue eyes sparkling with need.

He was badly tempted to go to her now, but how could he without making some kind of commitment?

Even thinking about moving in her direction, caused the snake to hiss, *You're not good enough, Duncan. You never will be. And she'll leave you. Women always leave.*

But even as the snake threatened to hurt him again, Rachel's scent suddenly rolled from the open door of the great room onto the patio. He rose to his feet, turning to face the living area, all his senses coming alive. The *breh-hedden* was taking a toll on them both, but he could tell Rachel had reached a new level of suffering.

And he had to accept the reality if he didn't take care of her, she'd find someone else who could.

Duncan.

Her voice was a pained whimper inside his head.

I'm here, he sent.

I need you. The desperate quality of her plea made up his mind.

He had to take care of his woman.

Though the snake kept hissing and his gut writhed, he lowered his chin and forced the sensations to subside. Rachel needed him and right now, nothing else mattered.

By the time he reached his master bedroom, Rachel's rich mating scent, so full of life, struck him like a blow to his chest. If he hadn't already made up his mind, he would have done so now.

She lay completely naked on the bed, face down, her hips grinding into the sheets, one hand extended between her legs and massaging. Her eyes were closed.

He crossed to her, losing his bottoms at the same time, his cock already firm.

"Rachel?"

She opened her eyes and gave a cry, turning onto her back and holding out her arms for him. She spread her legs and he saw how wet she was. "Duncan, thank God, I'm in agony. I don't know what's wrong with me."

He understood. "You're a warrior now. It comes with the territory and the *breh-hedden* isn't helping."

She nodded with three jerks of her chin. "I've just never felt like this before." Tears rolled from her eyes.

His arms shook as he positioned himself over her, settling his knees between her legs. Holding his cock in his hand, he pressed the crown against all her wetness and couldn't repress a heavy groan. He'd wanted to be with her a hundred times over the past month.

As he pushed his cock along her streaming well, she clutched at his shoulders. He lowered himself onto her and curled his hips. As Rachel tightened around him, the sweet fire that poured over his cock sent another groan from his lips.

Rachel was already panting, eyes closed, neck arched. Her fingers kneaded the muscles of his arms, digging her nails in. He moved his hips, driving his cock deep.

"Yes." Her breaths came light and quick. "So close. I've needed this."

He lifted up enough so he could see her face. He thrust in a quick, steady rhythm. She gasped repeatedly, her hands clutching him hard.

He'd just entered her and she was ready to come.

He knew her body, so he quickened his pace vampire fast.

"Duncan, my God!"

"Come for me, Rachel. Come now."

She gave out a long, low cry and he watched as ecstasy passed over her face. He sustained the pace, knowing it would give her pleasure. Leaning down, he kissed her neck, craving release, but holding his own orgasm at bay. As long as he focused on Rachel, he felt as though he could do anything.

Maybe he couldn't explain how much poison he had inside him, but right now, she had him.

When her orgasm crested and she began to relax, he slowed the movement of his hips until he finally stopped. He was surprised to find she was trembling, tears glistening in her eyes.

She lifted a hand and stroked his cheek. "Thank you. I honestly don't know what's wrong with me. And would it be too horrible if I asked you to keep going?"

He smiled down at her. "I'm here. Whatever you need, I'm here."

She ran a thumb over his lips. "Yes, you are."

He leaned close and kissed her. She opened for him and he took possession of her mouth the same way his cock had charge of her well.

While he kissed her, he moved his hips in a circle, letting every deep part of her feel how hard he was.

She gasped against his mouth, her breath sweet, the feel of her soft as he plunged his tongue in and out of her mouth, matching the movement with his cock.

I've needed you Duncan. Her voice within his head caused a euphoric sensation to roll through his mind.

I should have come to you sooner. I'm sorry Rachel. But I'm here now. Tell me what you want. I'll do anything, everything.

I love that you're kissing me. I feel more at ease yet revved up. Go faster.

He sped up the movement of his hips. *You're so wet for me. Can you feel me moving in and out of you?*

God, yes.

He went faster still. She gripped his shoulders, her abdomen tensing, her hips arching into his. She moved with him, then cried out.

Are you coming again? He asked. She'd always been easy to reach the peak, but even this second quick ascent surprised him.

Yes. Oh, Duncan.

Sustaining the drive of his hips, he drew back and watched as ecstasy once more took hold of her. More tears slipped from her eyes.

He dipped quickly to lick the dampness at the corner of her eye. *Even your tears taste like your garden.*

As her breathing settled, he slowed his hips until he finally stopped.

She caught his face with her hands. "Taste me between my legs, the way you used to."

He kissed her again. "Is that what you want?"

"Yes, please. Yes." She rolled her hips and he groaned. He wanted to let go, to drive into her hard and fill her full of his seed. But he needed to take care of her more than he needed a quick release. And when the moment arrived, he knew exactly how he wanted to come.

He kissed his way down her body, and would have suckled her nipples, but she stopped him. "The weapons harness has made me really sore. I'll toughen up eventually, just not right now."

He kept moving, taking time at her navel, using his tongue generously. He kept gliding lower, a thrill streaking through his balls at the thought of spending time with his tongue between her legs. He loved Rachel's sex, loved working her up.

He kissed her landing patch, his hands massaging her lower abdomen, her hips, and down the outsides of her thighs. He slid his tongue between her folds and began to stroke her in quick flicks, one of the ways she liked it.

Her hips jerked, telling him he'd found the right spot. His jaw trembled as he took turns sucking and dabbing at her, teasing her sex. She smelled rich and earthy, very Rachel, the woman he loved and wanted to love better.

He drifted his tongue lower to her opening, swirling and tasting. He loved how wet she was and how her flavors reminded him of her cottage garden. Maybe he couldn't tell her in words all he felt for her, but he let his tongue give full meaning to how much she meant to him.

He dipped inside, going as deep as he could, loving the intimate connection. He began to thrust.

She buried her hands in his hair, guiding him with a gentle but insistent pressure. Her hips rocked now, but he wanted a better position.

He left her well and moved backward to drop to the side of the bed. He pulled her hips close to the edge and angled her legs over his shoulders. Sliding his arms beneath her, he got going again, thrusting into her heavily. A series of cries left her throat. Her body writhed, then arched.

He moved faster and thrust harder until she was once more crying out. "Duncan, oh God!"

He worked her steadily, teasing the orgasm out as far as it would go until once more she'd reached the peak and relaxed into the mattress. He kissed the insides of her thighs.

She was breathing hard as she came back to earth.

He rose up so he could see her face. "You look so beautiful when you've come. In fact, you look more beautiful than ever, almost as though you're glowing."

She planted her hand on his chest and rubbed. More tears slid from her eyes. "Thank you, Duncan. I know this is hard for you."

He glanced down at his missile-like cock. "Definitely hard."

She chuckled. "And you could always make me laugh."

He frowned. "I'm sorry I've been a pain, but I still can't—"

"Hey. For what I need and for where the team is at, what you're doing right now is enough."

His gaze fell to her neck and he realized he was hungry for something more.

"Yes," she responded instantly, her lids falling to half-mast. "You need to feed. So, how do you want me, Duncan? On my stomach, maybe?" A slow smile curved her lips. She knew him so well.

"This is about you," he responded firmly. "Tell me what *you* want and I'll do it?"

She drifted her hand to his shoulder and squeezed. "I want you pounding into me and giving me everything you've got." When she followed this up by flipping over onto her stomach, his cock twitched and he sucked in some air.

Rising onto her knees, she crawled slowly toward the headboard. The sight of her sex, so beautifully swollen, had him gripping his cock as he followed after her.

He stroked her buttocks and would have reached around to fondle her breasts, but he remembered her earlier warning of being too tender to touch.

Instead, he leaned down and kissed his way up her back, sucking at the edge of each of her weeping wing-locks, then pushing her long blond hair to the side. He'd be biting her soon, but first, he positioned his hips behind her then eased his cock deep inside her well.

He licked her neck and she angled for him, giving him access to her waiting vein.

"So good," she whispered. "And Duncan?"

He kissed her throat, her cheek, the side of her mouth. "Yes."

"Take me hard. I need as much as you can give me. And when I said 'pounding', I meant it. Can't explain."

The invitation had his cock twitching again. He rose up for a moment and took her hips in hand. He pushed deep, thrusting the length of her over and over. "You feel amazing Rachel. I love doing this with you."

"Uh-huh." She moaned softly, her hips pushing back with each thrust.

~ ~ ~

Rachel couldn't really see anything, even though her eyes were open. She could only feel how hard Duncan was inside her and the force he used, which would increase in the next few minutes as he took her to the pinnacle again.

He'd already brought her over the edge several times, yet her hunger for him felt barely slaked. The *breh-hedden* had definitely arrived to rule her body.

When she felt Duncan bending over her, she stretched out her neck a little more, allowing him room for a clean breach.

She loved this part of the ascended world, that her body could be pierced in yet another way. Being a vampire had always felt right to her, the strike of the fangs, the sharing and taking of blood.

When she drank from Duncan, he now tasted just like his scent, a spicy ale, a gift of the *breh-hedden*. She would need his blood soon as well. But for now, feeding him seemed so much more important.

She could feel his saliva on her neck, a sure sign the strike would come soon.

He paused in the thrusts of his cock for a brief second, then bit with his fangs and began to suck. The thrill of having him drinking from her, swamped her with another layer of exquisite sensation. When he put his hips back in motion, his pistoning cock and suckling lips sent shivers chasing all over her body.

But it was something more, something almost spiritual as he took her blood: she nourished him with her life-force.

She began to pant and moan, her body on fire once more. In this position, her aching breasts swayed freely, adding a new layer of physical sensation.

Her well clenched as she drew close to yet another orgasm.

You're hard inside me, Duncan. So hard.

I love doing this with you. His deep voice within her mind made her clench once more. *I love your body and you're so tight, Rachel, stroking me just right. Your blood is an elixir down my throat. It's making me stronger. Have I told you as much? Even my muscles feel fired up. Here. Drink from me as well.*

She felt him shift, though still sustaining his thrusts, and the next moment he pressed his wrist to her mouth.

He was definitely strong enough to support himself on one arm as he held his wrist in position. He paused in his thrusts again and she groaned heavily as her own fangs descended. She struck the waiting collection of veins.

When his blood hit her mouth, she cried out.

If he moved, she wouldn't be able to sustain a proper seal, so he grew very still and let her have a good long drink. She sucked greedily, having missed his blood during the month of their separation. He sucked on her neck at the same time.

Her sex grew hot, swollen, and so needy all over again. He moved his hips in slow circles once more so she could feel him inside her.

Duncan, my God. I need to come. She released his wrist. "Take me hard, Duncan. Please."

He released her throat as well and rose up, gripping her hips in his hands and began to drive toward the finish.

That's when the real magic began with his cock working her deep. Using one hand, he stroked one of her wing-locks and she gasped. Duncan knew how to work her body.

The orgasm built and she opened up for it, letting the motion of his body drive the moment. He went even faster, grunting now, all man, all hard muscle and stiff cock as he pushed toward his release as well. His fingers pinched one of her wing-locks and for some reason, that brought the ecstasy flowing.

She cried out, all her attention fixed on the feel of the sweet, intense pleasure that began to release between her legs, rippling through her. At the same time, her wing-locks swelled and before she knew what was happening her wings-released, carrying her orgasm up through her abdomen and chest, flooding her heart with unbearable pleasure. She screamed her ecstasy.

She felt Duncan's hand between her wings, pressing her down in the middle of her back, keeping her grounded.

When he began to roar as he, too, released, all the sensations coalesced in yet another firestorm of pleasure that kept on rolling.

Shivers raced once more over her body. As her wings beat just at the tips, sensation upon sensation flowed up her back then down, gripping her between her legs. Wave after wave of pleasure rocked through her.

Finally, Duncan's thrusts began to slow and the intense cresting of passion gentled down. She grew very still, her wings resting to either side of her body. Her mind felt clouded and beautiful, her body finally satisfied and at ease. Still on hands and knees with Duncan connected from behind, she smiled. A feeling of peace descended over her like a warm blanket.

She knew Duncan had mounted his wings as well because a gentle breeze moved all around her.

Rachel, floated through her head. *I love you.*

I love you, too. She'd never doubted Duncan's love for her, only his ability to be in a relationship with her.

Right now however, she refused to get bogged down in any of their past issues. Instead, she focused on how wonderful she felt. Even her breasts didn't hurt nearly as much, which made her wonder if the lack of sex had contributed to their fiery ache.

After a moment, she drew in her wings and glanced back to watch Duncan's wafting in a slow, gentle rhythm.

She smiled. "My arms are about ready to give way."

He caressed her back with one hand. "Let me draw in my wings. I want to stay with you."

She knew what he meant. He didn't want to lose their intimate connection.

She nodded, her arms trembling. She could feel the movement of Duncan retracting his wings.

"All done," he whispered. "You can let go."

When Duncan surrounded her hips and abdomen with one arm, she lowered herself slowly. He stayed with her, keeping his cock buried deep. It would have been easy to glide out, but he'd always enjoyed staying inside her, something she'd loved about him.

When she stretched out her arms, he spread his on top of hers, as though they were flying together. Tears bit her eyes. She was so grateful to have had the release she'd needed, but her heart already ached, knowing the close connection couldn't last.

The viper living inside of Duncan would strike again soon.

Chapter Four

The future smiles

When the vision arrives on a swift-moving stream.

Collected Proverbs by **Beatrice of Fourth**

Duncan's veins flowed with Rachel's blood; he was still connected to her, and he'd taken care of her needs. For this brief moment, the world spun though the universe on exactly the right course. He even breathed more easily.

The terrible serpent, living in his gut, swam steadily but remained below the surface of the waters. He couldn't promise Rachel anything and she knew it. She didn't pressure him, either. But the lack of pressure carried its own force, pushing him to do better, though causing him to feel guilty when he didn't live up to expectations.

In a small way, his relationship with Rachel had changed. She no longer fought against him when he retreated. And he'd made an effort to help her understand what it was like for him, the devouring nature of the feelings that lived inside him, preventing him from moving forward.

Yet somehow, this morning he'd overcome the pain enough to do what needed to be done.

When he felt Rachel drifting off to sleep, he gently pulled out, tucked some tissues between her legs and covered her up. He knew she was exhausted.

She mumbled her thanks, even gripping his hand and kissing his fingers.

His heart pulled into a knot as he stared down at her. He didn't withdraw until the grip on his hand grew lax, her breathing evened out, and he knew she was falling asleep.

He stood over her for a long time, wishing he could fully understand what the hell was going on with him. The best he could figure was that his father's abuse coupled with his mother's forced abandonment, had warped him, had essentially made him feel broken and unworthy.

He pressed a hand to his stomach. The viper had already started moving again. All he had to do was invoke his father's memory and the serpent showed its fangs.

He shifted his focus to Rachel, the sex they'd shared, the blood, her patience with him.

Maybe Merl was right and he should seriously consider his relationship with Rachel in a new light. Was it possible the cessation of his visions had something to do with his inability to connect with her?

He thought about joining her in bed, but he wasn't ready for that. Instead, he showered again, returned to his guest bedroom and fell hard asleep.

When he woke up at dusk, he realized he'd slept better than he had anytime during the past month. He definitely needed to do whatever he could to move in Rachel's direction. He'd told her a few weeks ago he'd try and right now he made a new commitment to do just that.

As he sat up, however, a powerful dizziness overcame him and he flopped back down. He stared up at the ceiling, but the room moved around and he had to close his eyes.

He wasn't even sure he could get out of bed.

When lights started flashing over his eyelids, he knew he had to do something. At the very least, he needed to understand what was going on.

He opened his eyes once more, yet found it hard to breathe. He held his stomach; the viper was moving fast. But he couldn't let the old ways win anymore. He had to try. He couldn't let Rachel down again.

He forced himself to an upright position, supporting himself on one hand. The room still spun, but he had to get to Rachel.

Though the dizziness got worse, he struggled to his feet. He held onto the dresser and forced himself in the direction of the master bedroom. Fortunately, the more he moved, the better he felt. He crossed the living room and only had to pause once to keep his balance.

When he finally reached the master bedroom, he stopped inside the doorway and folded his sword into his right hand.

The dizziness increased to the point he thought he might fall. Had Yolanthe's wreckers finally found him?

"Rachel," he called to her in a strong voice.

She lifted her head and because she was lying on her stomach, she had to twist to meet his gaze. "Duncan, what's wrong?" She then rolled onto her back and pushed herself quickly to a sitting position.

The sheet fell away, revealing her full breasts. The male part of him took a long look, but he couldn't act on his ever-present desire for his woman. Instead, images began moving inside his head, one after the other in quick succession.

Then he understood. He was having his first vision in a month, though this one had come on stronger than anything he'd yet experienced.

But even as the images began to coalesce, he realized he didn't want another vision, he didn't want the gifts given to him. It was all too much, all at odds with his deepest beliefs of worthlessness. Then he understood how right Merl had been when he'd said Duncan had been holding back.

He just hadn't seen it until this moment.

As he stood with sword in hand in the doorway of his master bedroom, with Rachel looking beautiful and vulnerable on his bed, he knew he had a decision to make.

From the time Yolanthe had held him in a trance and he'd broken free in order to keep Rachel safe, he'd been building to this moment. Having a vision descend on him a few hours after making love to Rachel proved Merl's theory — Duncan's powers were connected to his relationship with Rachel.

He shifted slightly to meet her gaze. His fucked up life had always been about his love for Rachel and his inability to allow her in.

"Are you okay? What's going on?" She'd pulled the sheet up to cover herself. Her long, blond hair was in disarray and concern filled her blue eyes.

Could he go forward?

The viper lifted its head, fangs dripping with poison once more. And as doubt filled him, the approaching vision began to recede.

He made a quick grab for it, unwilling to let it disappear entirely, but his hold felt tenuous.

The snake within his gut moved swiftly now.

Rachel called out, "Duncan, you're scaring me."

He couldn't respond; he could only reach deep inside and press the snake's head down beneath the waters, trying to subdue it.

One of his father's favorite taunts rolled through Duncan's mind: *You're not good enough, my son. You'll never be a real warrior. Your test will come and you'll fail. Then you'll remember I was always right about you. You're weak like your mother.*

But Duncan was a warrior, a powerful one. And he'd exceeded his father, who'd never reached Warrior of the Blood level. Yet Duncan had. For this reason alone, he knew his father's words were a lie.

He glanced at the sword which he still held aloft. The bright metal glowed. His gaze ran down his body and a slight trail of smoke with a faint bluish hue began to rise into the air. Holy shit, he was looking at *grayle* power, a Third Earth ability. Somehow he'd accessed it or maybe having a vision at this level had opened up his *grayle* ability.

Still, he held back. He didn't know all he'd be facing once he embraced the powers that seemed ready to flow within him.

Turning toward Rachel and ignoring the terrible pain that lived inside him, he knew he had to choose. Should he embrace the vision and move forward, or should he retreat into a life he understood, of repressing the pain of his growing up years and of never getting close to anyone?

But as he peered into the future, one thought rose above all others: he didn't want to be a slave to the past. He wanted to be more than he was and apparently, every other part of his life was ready take the leap. All this power had come to him unbidden and a beautiful, worthy woman loved him despite his flaws.

He knew then he couldn't go back and as painful as the future promised to be, he wanted to be part of the team, to have visions that could aid in battle, and dammit, he wanted to share his life and his bed with Rachel.

With that, he lifted his sword higher still and let the vision come.

~ ~ ~

Uncertain what was happening, Rachel stared at Duncan. "Duncan?"

No response.

Oh, shit, what now?

She listened for the faint rumbles of an approaching grid incursion that would usher in the sudden presence of Third Earth wreckers and their sawed-off shotguns. But she didn't hear anything.

Just in case Duncan's current state meant the wreckers had a bead on them, she slipped from bed and folded a wrecking gun into her hand. As a quick after thought, she added a box of ammo from Duncan's weapons locker. She quickly loaded the gun, then moved to stand in front of Duncan. She faced into the room, with her back to Duncan and listened hard for the enemy. But no sounds returned to her.

"Duncan?"

Still no response.

Whatever had caught him up, she'd just have to wait it out.

After a couple of minutes, she stepped several feet away from him and turned to face him. They were both completely naked, yet somehow the absence of clothes seemed fitting after great sex, a good night's sleep, and now some kind of ascended phenomenon that held Duncan in a trance.

She thought of Yolanthe and a dart of fear raced through her. Had the woman found Duncan again and set up another mind-link?

Rachel doubted it since the last two times she'd seen Duncan entranced, he'd been knocked to a prone position.

Right now, he stood upright, shoulders back, his sword held high. He had a magnificent physique, his pecs thick and muscled, his arms bulked, hips narrow, thighs heavy and ripped, his stomach a true six-pack. Something from Greek mythology, maybe.

And he glowed.

A warm light emanated from his entire body. He also had a stream of *grayle* smoke, with a bluish hue streaming from his body.

As she took in the signs, she knew he had to be in the middle of a vision.

Her heart set up a noisy racket, thumping loudly in her ears. Duncan hadn't had a vision in a month, now here he was, caught up in one and bearing his sword.

She took a moment to settle into herself and to calm her heart. He would need protection in his current state. As powerful as he was, the enemy could still strike him down.

Her shielding instincts kicked in. She could have drawn close to release what Merl had told her was her Fourth Earth ability. Given she heard no warning rumbles, she decided to take the opportunity to practice and instead moved twelve feet away from him.

She let her power flow and a warm vibration of energy moved

through her, extending quickly toward Duncan. She knew the split-second he was completely covered by her shield. She felt very secure with her power and with her shotgun in hand, she stood guard.

~ ~ ~

Duncan knew he was caught in a vision and that he stood fully exposed to attack. But he had a profound sense of peace, which probably meant Rachel had shielded him.

Within the vision, he levitated and travelled slowly through the Third darkening grid. The vision had a dreamlike quality yet every detail was sharp and clear.

Within the vision, the grid had a familiar feel, as though he knew it well, especially when he reached an arched portal that glowed. He glanced down at what he could see was a wrist scanner and watched as his fingers punched in a series of numbers. These, he memorized, knowing they were a secret code.

The portal opened and he passed through, still levitating. He moved into a dark space made of gray stone blocks, and he knew exactly where he was; Sharav had tortured him in this place.

To the right was a curved stone staircase leading to a ground floor and to the left a long row of prison cells. The first one was empty. Here, he'd been jailed and tortured, his powers brought forward from the effort of battling Sharav's mind-control.

He knew now that Sharav had purposely hurt him, intending to jump-start his Third Earth powers.

The vision took him momentarily into the past and he was back in the cell, his body on fire. This time, he was able to open his eyes and he could see Yolanthe. She'd been present through part of his torture, her pale blue eyes lit with a fanatical light. She looked different back then because her hair hadn't been in braids.

Yolanthe drew close to Sharav, caressing his arm. "His powers are expanding, aren't they?"

"Yes, like Samuel's. But I haven't brought his *grayle* power forward yet. Given time, though, I know I will."

Within the vision, Duncan blinked and he pulled out of the cell. He shuddered at the memory of so much pain. Though Yolanthe had been there from the beginning, this was the first time he'd actually seen her as part of the torture process. She must have forged her mind-link during this period since he would have been unable to withstand her in such a weakened state.

So, he'd been in her plans for some time and it was all about finding Rapture's Edge.

He began floating down the hall. Most of the cells contained powerful, warrior-like men, each with long braids at the sides of their face. The men were shackled and in despair. How long had they been there?

Those facing the wall had identical black tattoos running down the center of their spines, indicating a shared purpose. Instinctively, he knew he was looking at Third Earth Warriors of the Blood. Despite their stature, he knew he wasn't there for them.

Instead, he felt a powerful pull from the very last cell and he sped up until he reached the barred space.

A woman sat on a cot, wearing a long, white linen gown and a strange, semi-sheer lavender veil over her head. The veil had small metal weights around the bottom, keeping it in place. Her hands were free so she could have removed the veil, yet she didn't.

He tried to speak to her, but no sound would leave his throat. She turned toward him anyway, then rose to her feet. "Is someone there? Tell me, please."

He wanted to answer her, but couldn't.

He felt desperate to communicate, and within the vision he tried to reach her telepathically. *I'm Duncan of Second Earth. Who are you?*

Thank the Creator your telepathic powers are so strong. She moved toward him. *But you're not really there. You feel like a ghost.*

I'm not a ghost.

Duncan, you must help me if you can. I'm in danger. Yolanthe intends to destroy all of us within the next few days. I've seen it in the future streams.

What's your name?

But before she could answer, he heard shouting at a distance. He looked back up the long hall. The warriors in the cells had started calling to each other at the same time. From the stone staircase, he heard running footsteps and the next moment, Third Earth Militia Warriors swarmed the space.

He felt jerked backward through the vision and kept flying back and back as through a long tunnel. *I'll do what I can,* he sent, though he had no idea if the woman could hear him.

Reconnecting with his body on Second Earth, it took a moment for him to even open his eyes. When he did, Rachel was there with her back to him. She was guarding him just as he knew she would be. She even held a wrecker shotgun in her hand.

He felt as he often did when he woke up from a nightmare — the urgency of the dream clinging to him like a second skin.

The woman in the vision was critical to the war on Third. He felt it in his bones. He had no idea who she was except that she had Seer ability and Yolanthe held her captive and veiled.

He glanced down at his fist, still holding the grip of his sword. He knew only one thing; the black ops team had to rescue the woman, whose name he still didn't know, within the next few days.

"Rachel?"

She turned around, her large blue eyes wide. "You're back."

"How long was I gone?"

"Ten, fifteen minutes. Don't worry; I shielded you."

He nodded. "I know." He glanced at the shotgun she held in her hands.

She drew close and laid her hand on his left arm. She searched his eyes. "A vision?"

As though his brain still worked to catch up, words didn't come right away. He inclined his head as portions of the vision replayed through his mind. He folded his sword to his weapons locker and slid an arm around her shoulders, pulling her close. She sent the shotgun away at the same time.

Everything was changing, including his relationship with Rachel, whether he could handle it or not. He felt her sigh as she slid both arms around his waist and hugged him. "You're back."

"I am."

"Something has changed, though, hasn't it?" she asked.

"Yes. I'm not going to pull away from you this time, but I'll need your help. Something inside me is tearing me apart and I don't know how to fix it."

"I'll do whatever you need me to do, Duncan. You're worth the effort, do you understand?"

He nodded, knowing she'd touched the heart of the issue. "I love you," he whispered.

She lay her head against his shoulder and sighed once more. "Are you okay?"

"I am."

"Can you tell me what you saw?"

With his arms holding her tight he shared the vision, beginning to end.

~ ~ ~

As Duncan spoke, Rachel could feel his heart beating and the sound mesmerized her. His whole body was warm, no doubt from the energy flowing through him which had produced the glow. She wanted to stay with her arms around him forever, just like this, skin-to-skin, resting against him, hearing the steady beat of his heart.

He spoke of a prison, of Third Earth What-Bees and Militia Warriors aligned with Yolanthe, and of a veiled woman desperate to get out of her cell. He also believed the vision had led him to Yolanthe's prison because of Rapture's Edge.

As his description ended, he made no move to let her go so she stayed and held him. Suddenly, the vision began to roll through her mind as well. *I'm seeing the vision, Duncan.*

You are?

Yes. As the vision played through, she described it to him telepathically, moment by moment, including the numbered sequence at the portal. He was astonished by her descriptions.

That was amazing, she sent, as the veiled woman disappeared from sight. Aloud, she said, "And I can feel her connection to Rapture's Edge. We're meant to rescue her, aren't we?"

"Yes. That's exactly what we're supposed to do."

She drew away from him slightly. "How?"

At that, he smiled and seemed more like himself. "I have no idea."

"Then we'd better get the team together."

As he moved away from her, his gaze drifted down her body and his lids fell low.

She nodded, licking her lips. If he offered to take her to bed right now, she wouldn't say no despite the need to get going.

"Your scent," he whispered, drawing close once more and kissing the top of her head.

"Can't help it."

He shifted as she lifted her face to his. He kissed her, a deep, warm kiss that made her heart pound with hope and desire.

"The bed is right here." She drew back just enough to hold his gaze. She kissed him again so he didn't really have sufficient time to answer.

She could feel his cock growing firm against her abdomen. She rubbed back and forth.

He quickly drew away from her, however, then caught her chin with his hand. "I'd want nothing more than to make love to you again, but there's an urgency about this vision. And you're right, we need to inform the team."

"I know."

He kissed her once more, then turned and headed to the guest room.

She put a hand to her chest, breathing hard, and all he'd done was kiss her. She didn't mind that he'd left because the view of his tight ass, broad shoulders, and warrior's gate would keep her revved up until the time was right.

She wasn't a fool; nothing had been resolved. Whatever had burrowed into Duncan's psyche and held him captive, wouldn't be letting go anytime soon.

But God help her, she would do everything she could to encourage his steps in her direction.

The fact that a vision had followed after they'd been together for the first time in a month, she took as a powerful sign to stay the course.

~ ~ ~

With a wave of his hand, Duncan folded on his battle uniform. Renewed energy flowed through him in a vibrating wave of power. He knew how much his vision would intensify the team's purpose and immediate direction, and for reasons he couldn't explain, he also sensed the content would cause Merl a profound degree of distress.

He was about to contact Luken, when Merl became fixed in Duncan's mind not as an obstacle, but as something else, something more. He'd been so enraged by the Third ascender's shitty attitude, he hadn't stopped to consider the man who had once served as a Warrior of the Blood on Third.

Questions rose to mind, mostly why Merl had lived his life as an exile on Second. He'd always bought Merl's story that he'd pissed off a few powerful entities and had gotten cast out as a result. It wasn't hard to believe; Merl could rub anyone the wrong way.

But what if it was something else, something much more significant which had sent Merl to Second?

As he reached for his cell, one more issue surfaced. If the team was going to have the smallest chance of battling on Third, they had to have a boost in power. Now.

The team needed Warrior Jean-Pierre, the Frenchman who'd folded straight off the guillotine during the harshest part of the French Revolution. He was *breh*-bonded to Fiona and had gained a phenomenal ability to help others gain power. Before Duncan's abduction, Jean-Pierre had been working with him to bring his visions forward.

Right now, however, they'd need him round the clock until the team was brought up to speed.

Duncan made his call to Luken, who in turn didn't hesitate to contact Jeannie at Central Command to get the meeting set up. Luken felt confident Jean-Pierre would be willing to devote all his time to the black ops team. He was in high demand since Endelle had ordered him to bring as many Militia Warriors as possible into their emerging powers for the critical war effort on Second.

With the plan in motion, Duncan crossed to the master bedroom and found Rachel drying her hair. She wore a turquoise silk robe that clung to her curves.

"We're a go," he said. "Luken worked his magic."

Rachel shut off her hair dryer and began brushing out her hair. "Jeannie?"

Duncan smiled. "Who else? She adores him." Jeannie and Carla kept communication moving strong among all the warriors.

"When do we leave?" Rachel pulled her hair into a ponytail and secured the *cadroen,* a dark brown leather clasp with a bone pin that all the Warriors of the Blood used.

"We can leave whenever you're ready. We'll be heading to Jean-Pierre's home in Sedona."

At that, she turned to him. "Really? I've never been there." She shook her head. "Any particular reason?"

"Jean-Pierre said he's had recent success using the central room in his house. Not sure why. But I think you'll like his home. It's set in a grove of Arizona sycamores and he built the entire structure himself using hand tools."

She shifted her gaze away from him and nodded slowly, but he couldn't mistake the sadness in her eyes.

He understood. "I'm sorry about your home, Rachel."

She huffed a sigh, waved a hand, and switched out her robe for her black leather flight suit. The male warriors had adopted kilts a long time ago. But the female warriors preferred a flight suit with snug leather pants and a weapons harness. All battle harnesses had a strip of leather down the spine to allow for wing-mount.

With her small waist and full hips, Rachel looked especially good in her suit. Sudden desire flowed and without thinking, he put his feet in motion, intending to haul her into his arms.

By the time he reached her, however, she'd bent over at the waist and was wincing.

"What's the matter?"

She flipped the side tabs on the harness. "I'm still chafing and it's really bugging me. Can you help me adjust the harness? I've let it out twice now, but it's still not right."

"Of course." He stepped close and according to her instructions, loosened the side straps so that when the closing mechanisms were snapped shut, she'd have more room.

It took a few minutes, but when he was done, she released a huge sigh. "Oh, thank God. That feels a thousand times better."

"Didn't you have this adjusted when you first put it on?"

"Yes. And it fit well at first, but lately—" She didn't finish the

67

sentence. "Never mind. It's not important." She put the hair dryer away and turned off the bathroom light. After testing the daggers in her harness twice, she asked, "Are you ready?"

He smiled, thinking how much she'd changed. But the real question hit him all over again. With the viper filling him with poison, could he really be part of her life?

He ground his jaw. Somehow he had to make this work.

"Let's go."

~ ~ ~

Yolanthe paced the south terrace of her Mexico City Three home. She felt uneasy as she rubbed the back of her neck, then stroked the three thin braids hanging to her shoulder. She had a comfortable microclimate established over her property, so nothing but a lovely, balmy breeze blew through the villa palace.

Yet, she could not be content. Something nagged at her and with a sudden swamp of intuition, she knew she had to pay one of her permanent guests a visit.

She was about to head down to her prison, when she heard footsteps. Turning in the direction of the south terrace, she saw her brother walking in her direction, his usual quirky smile on his lips.

She adored Zander, both as her brother and in many ways as though she'd given birth to him herself. The twisted hump of his wings gave him an awkward gait, but he was no less beloved in her eyes.

Her heart warmed as she moved toward him, her arms held out. Her silks rustled softly about her legs. She wore a lavender underdress because Zander had complimented her on the color the last time she'd worn it. The fabric had a soft shimmer of gold embroidered throughout.

Her sleeveless over-gown was of deep purple, though lighter than her dark lipstick.

He took her arms, gripping her to the elbow, then leaned in to kiss her on each cheek. His silvery-blue eyes twinkled with good humor.

Though she'd known him all but ten of her nine-hundred-years, it still surprised her how much he resembled their father, Chustaffus. He had the same aquiline nose and broad cheeks, even a sweet dimple in his chin. He could do no wrong in her eyes, and it was for him she'd settled on acquiring Rapture's Edge. If she could offer the property to her father, and share how Zander had been instrumental in helping her obtain it, then Chustaffus might accept and embrace his deformed son.

More than anything, she wanted Zander brought into the warlike bosom of her family.

In the same way he held her elbows, she gripped his forearms. "So, tell me, brother, do you have word from the future streams about our miscreant?"

"You mean Duncan?" His eyes twinkled a little more.

"Of course I mean Duncan." She sighed.

"You've been crushing on him, sister."

"I will not deny I'd been looking forward to taking him into my baths and making ample use of his warrior body. For that reason alone, I'm hoping you have word of him."

At that, he released her arms and led her back to her *chaise*. "Ah, I see you've ordered my favorite wine." Zander loved a sweet Elderberry wine spiced with cinnamon and cloves.

She knew him well and by his demeanor and tone of voice, she also knew he didn't have good news for her. When he sat in the chair she'd had made to accommodate his wing-humps, she poured him a glass and handed it to him.

She preferred a chocolate wine herself and taking her already prepared glass with her, she sat down on her cream *chaise-longue*. "Are you still unable to find Duncan in the streams?"

He held the stemmed glass by the base and slowly swirled his wine. "I'm afraid not." He shook his head, frowning. "I spent six hours hunting through the future streams this morning. Once in a while, I could feel myself drawing close to Duncan, especially when I focused on some of the warriors with whom he has served in recent decades, all Militia Warriors: Owen, Joshua and Alex. But just as I was making progress and could sense Duncan wasn't far away, I lost all of them. And not one of my substantial powers could summon them back."

Yolanthe leaned forward, frowning. "This is very odd."

Zander nodded. "I can only draw one conclusion: I'm being blocked by another powerful Seer."

"But how would that be possible? Our father has the most powerful Seers on Third Earth bound in his Seers Fortress in Chicago Three."

"I had the same thought. But I'm reporting what I've experienced and I'm telling you a Third Earth Seer is blocking access to your man."

Her man. Duncan and those green eyes. His hair was thick and to his shoulders. How many times had she imagined sliding her fingers through his hair, drifting down to his neck and sinking her nails. With just a few thoughts of him, she felt a profound need to head to her baths, which she would do once she visited her prisoner.

She sipped her chocolate wine and repressed a heavy sigh. She could only conclude her brother had it right for no other reason than Duncan existed. She couldn't be the only one seeking Rapture's Edge, so others would know of Duncan as well. But who would this entity possibly be? She wondered if The Prince, who ruled a third of the planet, was also after Rapture's Edge, but she doubted it. He was far too busy holding off an infinite number of rebellions to be hunting for either Duncan or Rapture's Edge.

Sipping her wine, she added, "Keep trying, my love."

"I will. You may trust me in that."

"I do. All we need is one small opening and I will set my Mexican Three army after him."

"Even the death vampires?"

"Of course. I will not rest until I have Duncan back under my control."

Chapter Five

Change can kiss my ass.

Favorite Sayings – **Madame Endelle, Supreme High Administrator of Second Earth**

Luken smiled as Rachel took tentative steps across the thick glass floor of Jean-Pierre's 'sycamore' room. The glass allowed a view of Oak Creek below, though the room was open to the night sky above.

The forty-foot space was a perfect circle with no windows on the paneled redwood walls. The central tree had an odd horizontal and very low branch jutting from the main trunk, something Jean-Pierre must have trained early on in the tree's life. A certain amount of gossip had made the rounds about the branch. By the height of it, Luken knew the gossip was probably true.

Poor Fiona. She would blush scarlet for a year if she knew how much their community of warriors and their *breh* had actually discussed the tree in this room.

Yet something about the space, and the potential use for the branch between a man and his woman, made Luken's heart tighten. His lips parted and he drew a breath that felt centuries old. He couldn't remember the last time he'd had a serious relationship. Maybe never. Havily had been the closest thing in recent centuries. But even then, she'd never truly belonged to him. Long before her *breh,* Marcus, had come along, he'd asked Havily out repeatedly. But she'd always refused for the simple reason she knew she could never reciprocate his feelings.

71

He hadn't seen her in a month, not since his last visit to her office at Endelle's administrative HQ opposite Camelback Mountain Two. What surprised him was how little his thoughts had returned to her during the ensuing weeks. Even his desperate longings for her had dimmed in the face of his new mission.

He concluded that what had been a century of unrequited love had at long last come to an end, though he couldn't say why. But his eyes faced forward now, settled strongly on Third Earth. He felt as though he'd sailed away on a ship intended for a very long voyage.

And in his heart, he wished Havily and Marcus well.

The door to the room opened, drawing his eye away from the branch. But what a shock when Endelle walked in. For one thing, he hadn't been expecting her. For another, she looked like she was made for … nope, he didn't know what she was made for.

All eyes turned her direction.

Endelle had traded in her scorpion motif and now wore a breastplate of small, blade-like shapes made of brass, each dotted with a cluster of red, green and blue crystals. There had to be thirty of them forming a plate that flowed to a point that hit her bare navel. She wore a sheer, cloud-like red skirt hanging from her hips to mid-calf, made out of some kind of mesh fabric. A skimpy red slip beneath covered the tops of her hips and ran to another point, hiding her womanly bits. Otherwise the bare sides of her hips were visible through the sheer fabric of the skirt.

And of course she wore stiletto boots that hit her above the knee.

Endelle had always looked like an Arabian princess, no less so now with her thick, black hair teased into a massive volume and studded with three peacock feathers.

She had to dip below the doorway just to enter the room. She was tall for a woman anyway at six-five, but her stilettos and feathers put her over the top. She looked absurd yet regal at the same time, vintage Endelle.

"Jeannie called and told me you were meeting at Jean-Pierre's home. Thought I should be here." She frowned as her gaze slid around the group. "So what's going on?"

It struck Luken the woman rarely frowned. She yelled, shouted, and spoke with a resonance that hurt his ears, but generally her face maintained a less involved and quite beautiful expression.

"It's about Duncan's vision," he said.

Her brows rose. "No fucking shit." Her gaze shifted to Duncan and she acknowledged him with a slow dip of her chin. "So you've finally opened up a passage to the future again."

"Yes, Ma'am."

Luken expected Endelle to begin grilling Duncan on the details. Instead, she turned her attention back to Luken, fixing her unusual wooded brown gaze on him. Then, without saying another word, or making even one snide comment, she crossed to stand beside him.

He wondered if she knew she'd been doing that a lot lately, taking up a position next to him, side-by-side. So, what the hell was going on with Endelle? It was as though the whole team had been thrown up into the air and he wasn't sure where any of them would land.

Owen, Joshua, and Alex leaned against the horizontal branch, and each stared at Endelle, brows lifted, eyes moving to take in the sum total of her outfit.

But after a moment, each man looked away. Though there was a ridiculous element to the warrior-type costume, it was also sexy as hell. None of the men wanted to be lusting after their leader. It wasn't right.

Merl, not surprising, hung back from the group, his broad, muscular shoulders planted against the redwood wall. He held an unlit cigarette between his fingers and didn't even look at Endelle; he didn't look at anyone. The brother was damn lost. He was here, yet he wasn't, and it irritated the hell out of Luken because he still didn't know what was going on with Merl.

Rachel stood beside Duncan, her expression intrigued as she looked

Endelle over. She didn't smile or smirk and he liked that about Rachel. She was a good woman and now a dedicated warrior. She also looked better than she had the night before. And as Luken glanced at Duncan, he could see the brother was more relaxed and was now sticking close to Rachel. Both circumstances led Luken to believe the couple might have made some kind of peace, which was a good thing. The entire team had felt the difficult tension between the couple.

As a new thought occurred to him, Luken stood up a little straighter. The *breh-hedden* was a mystery in his world and from the first had been connected to the emerging powers of the couple involved. If Duncan had shared his bed with Rachel, was that the reason he'd suddenly had a vision? Even Merl had suggested the failure of Duncan's gift had been a result of his discord with his woman.

And that would be something to consider as he continued building his team, especially if more women entered the picture. Given the history of the *breh-hedden* and its march through the Warriors of the Blood, he had no reason to believe it wouldn't happen to the ops team as well, Rachel and Duncan being a prime example.

But it was time to get things moving, so he called out. "We're all here, Duncan. What have you got for us?"

As Duncan began to speak, an odd vibration passed through the room, a wave of power that made the hair on Luken's neck stand up. Duncan spoke of a portal in the Third grid and a sequence of numbers that took him straight into Yolanthe's prison, the place where Duncan had been tortured.

The more he spoke and gave himself to recounting the vision to the team, dammit if Duncan's body didn't start to glow. Even Merl pushed away from the wall, his attention caught. Luken was pretty sure Merl mouthed the word 'shit' a couple of times.

This had to be the *grayle* power Merl kept talking about similar to what Warrior Samuel now possessed. As a bluish stream of smoke left

Duncan's body, it was clear Duncan had finally made at least one leap to Third Earth ability.

"Well, look at that," Endelle murmured. "Holy fucking shit."

"Yeah. It's the *grayle* power."

Luken took a deep breath. He wanted to feel hopeful, but this group was a long way from functioning as a unit. Duncan and Rachel had their ongoing issues, the rest of his team had gotten stuck at Second Earth What-Bee levels, and of course Merl was a goddam island.

When Duncan finished laying out the vision, Luken said, "But who is this veiled woman?"

Duncan said he had no idea. The vision hadn't offered up a name or told him any details about her.

He shifted slightly and addressed Merl, "Do you know who she might be?"

Merl shrugged, then snorted. "How the hell should I know?"

Something snapped inside Luken. He'd had it with Merl's insolence. Half-folding, half-running, Luken crossed the distance to Merl then landed his fist against his jaw. Caught off guard, the brother slid across and down the redwood paneled wall, landing on his ass. He glared up at Luken.

Joshua didn't withhold his approval. "That should teach the bastard."

Luken stood over Merl. "I've had enough of your shit. Pull it together. And yes, you might have a helluva lot more power than me, but I'm your goddam superior officer and I'm telling you to either quit the team right now or get over yourself."

Merl glowered at Luken, his light blue eyes dark in the dimness of the chamber. With his Third Earth abilities, he could have taken Luken down to cinders. Instead, he showed respect by remaining where he was, on the floor, his jaw swelling. He settled his hand over the bruise and from the vibrations in the air, Luken knew Merl had started the self-healing process.

Endelle had moved with Luken and now flanked him on his left.

Though he felt her anger revving up, to Luken's surprise, she didn't let loose; she was leaving this up to him.

Luken continued, "Once and for all, Merl, I need you to lose the attitude. You've been like a bear with a pack of wolves at your heels. What the hell is going on with you?"

Merl slid his gaze to Endelle, then made a once around the group. Luken glanced as well and saw that the entire team had formed a half-circle. Was there one of them who didn't have a beef with Merl?

He leaned his head against the redwood wall. He'd never looked more despondent.

Much to Luken's shock, tears filled Merl's eyes. He glanced up at Luken. "Do you have a sister?"

The question took Luken so much by surprise, that for a moment he couldn't respond. Yes, he had a sister, but he had no idea if she was still alive. Centuries ago, in order to save her from their sadistic father, he'd spirited her away from the Norse lands so she'd have a chance at surviving. He hadn't seen or heard from her since. "I do, or I did. It's been a long time since I saw her."

"Do you still think about her?"

Luken debated for a moment whether to speak the truth to the entire group since no one knew, not even Endelle. But it seemed to him that Merl might open up a little if he went first. "Last thing at night, first thing in the morning." He felt the team's focus turn toward him, but he kept his attention fixed on Merl.

The brother nodded. "Then we have something in common." He waited for a moment, before saying, "There are two things you have to know. First, my grid signature will show up the moment I step foot on Third Earth and I'll be hunted down by either Chustaffus's or Yolanthe's forces. And second," he swiped a tear from his face, his lips turned down. "Yolanthe has kept my sister imprisoned for the past fifty years, the price of my exile. She'll kill Katlynn if I return to Third."

"Sweet merciful Creator," Alex murmured.

Owen stepped forward, his jaw grinding. "Do you think the veiled woman is your sister? Is that what you're saying?"

Merl nodded, his eyes red-rimmed. "I think she has to be Katlynn." His voice sounded flat, hopeless.

Almost as one, the group drew closer to Merl, who remained sitting on the floor. To no one's surprise, he held out his hand and with one of his Third tricks, lit the cigarette he still held between his fingers, without any visible means of doing it. He took a long, slow drag. "So you see, we're fucked on more than one level."

Jean-Pierre stood on the other side of Endelle. "All this time," he said, his French accent softening his words, "You've lived in fear of your sister being harmed by the same maniac that held Duncan in a trance?"

Merl nodded.

"*Mon dieu.*"

Endelle made an angry scoffing sound at the back of her throat. "Why the fuck didn't you tell us sooner? You know us, Merl. We're good people."

"I'm in violation of my agreement with Yolanthe right now because I've told you about Katlynn." He rose to his feet and took another drag, his eyes skittering about as though seeking the solution to an unsolvable problem.

Luken now understood everything about Merl, in part because he knew what it was to love a sibling and to live in fear for her safety. His own sister would always have part of his heart. "Where is Yolanthe's prison?"

Merl shook his head. "I'm not sure, but my guess has always been Mexico City Three. Her palace compound is one of the best fortified on Third Earth. It appears to be all gardens, lagoons and waterways, but it's a citadel, covered in an impenetrable mist the woman created herself. And she has a standing army of Militia Warriors completely devoted to her, as well as a lot death vamps, all on the property."

"How many warriors in her army?" Luken asked.

Merl shook his head. "At least five hundred on her estate alone. But why the fucking questions? You think you're going to bust the veiled woman out of this prison, whether she's my sister or not?"

Luken glanced at Duncan who offered a single dip of his chin.

Luken couldn't explain the level of certainty that overcame him despite Merl's doubt, but he went with it. "That's exactly what we're going to do and you're wrong, you will go to Third Earth with us. You're one of us now. Duncan's vision has given us the security code to the portal leading straight into the prison. We can do this, as limited as we are. We can do it. And we'll use your portal for entrance onto the grid. The rest, we'll figure out as we go, including your vulnerability on Third. But we're meant to do this."

Merl nodded. He might not appear completely convinced, but he'd lost some of his despair.

Luken turned to Duncan. "And this woman, possibly Katlynn, said she had only a few days to live. Right?"

"The warriors as well."

Luken frowned. "Wait, what warriors? You mean the men in the cells."

"Yes. I'm certain all seven men were Third Earth Warriors of the Blood."

Merl turned toward Duncan, his face paling dramatically. "You have to be mistaken. I mean, how could you know these men are What-Bees?"

"Because of the nature of the vision. They seemed to be a team as well since each of the men had the same tattoo running down his spine."

Merl weaved on his feet, and uttered a string of curses. He then stunned them all by folding off his maroon battle harness and turning around. His back was fully exposed. "A tattoo like this one?"

Luken nodded to Duncan. "Is this what you saw in the vision?"

The black tattoo was composed of a long line of stacked blade points, traveling from a broader design at the top where the harness formed a T at the neck. At the base was a similar configuration to the initial one, but wider.

"Exactly," Duncan said. "There's no doubt in my mind. This is the tattoo I saw in the vision."

Merl turned around slowly to face Duncan, but his gaze now had a wild, almost panicked look. "Not my men. She fucking promised me. Yolanthe said she'd leave them in peace if I left Third." A keening sound came from his throat. It was a high screech that slowly descended in timbre and turned into a resonant roar.

The team backed swiftly away from him as he began to pace. He folded and levitated, shouting his rage. Somewhere in the middle of moving around, his wings launched, the lavender and black bands taking him into the air. He flew erratically near the branches of the sycamore. All the while his agonized voice raged.

Luken felt a breeze next to him, the first clue Endelle had mounted her wings as well. She could change their color whenever she liked, one more instance of her enormous power, and right now they were a deep red. She rose into the air and began to track beside Merl. At this distance, beneath Merl's pained roars, Luken heard Endelle's voice as she began talking him down.

Luken joined Jean-Pierre and the rest of the team as they moved to stand close to the redwood paneled walls, getting out of the way. No one said a word, but a terrible vibration of pain had filled the entire room.

Somewhere in midair, Merl finally drew in his wings and levitated close to Endelle. To everyone's surprise, she surrounded the powerful warrior with her arms, supporting them both with the waft of her own wings. The man's ensuing sobs tore Luken to shreds.

Luken turned to Jean-Pierre. "Got any beer in your fridge?"

"*Oui*, of course."

Luken gestured for the team to file out. No one protested.

~ ~ ~

Rachel wasn't as surprised as she might have been that Merl lost it. Through the vision Duncan had shared with her, she'd seen the warriors chained up, no doubt tortured as well. If the veiled woman was his sister and if his fellow warriors had been imprisoned despite his efforts to save them, it was no wonder he'd taken it hard.

Because of Rachel's brother, Gideon, and his warrior-like qualities, she'd been around fighting men her entire life. She understood them, the camaraderie, the depth of devotion each had to the land they defended, the unspoken commitment to never leave a man behind, the love they held for each other.

Apparently, Merl had left seven of his brothers-in-arms behind as well as his sister. It was also clear Yolanthe had lied to Merl. She'd taken Merl's team when she'd promised to leave them alone.

Her own throat tightened at the sight of Endelle holding Merl in her arms. Her massive scarlet wings wafted slowly, keeping her in place and away from the upper canopy branches. Rachel took Duncan's hand in a tight grip.

These men gave everything they had in service to others. They battled hard, trained their bodies mercilessly, and were prepared to lay down their lives. Merl had lived in the cold for five decades, not knowing the fate of either his sister or his brother-warriors.

His prior behavior became clear to her, why he'd acted as though he didn't care about anything but his own pleasure and why he'd held back being part of Luken's team. He'd been a man sustaining a façade to protect those he loved. He'd been nothing but warrior, after all.

Yet, seeing Merl so completely destroyed brought the war home to Rachel in a way it hadn't during the past month of training. She'd made a transition, a big one, to Warrior of the Blood. She battled beside the men, making use of her shield ability, the occasional use of a wrecker shotgun, and her finesse with daggers.

But she'd forgotten the other side, the one of personal destruction.

Luken began waving them toward the door, no doubt intending to give Merl some space. She put her feet in motion, her hand still tucked within Duncan's. She had no idea what he was thinking, but her own reaction had put her back in the past without warning.

There were many reasons she'd fought against joining up with the Ops Team. The main one had involved Grieg, her abusive husband, now deceased. Not that she was excusing Grieg's behavior, but the warrior life took a toll on the men and women who served.

Did she really want that life for herself? She'd made a commitment to serve on the team because she knew this was where she belonged, at least for the present. She'd be offering her shielding protection to Duncan and the rest of the team repeatedly over the coming weeks, perhaps even months. And she'd be saving lives.

But how could this ever be a lifetime endeavor for her?

You okay? Duncan sent.

I don't know.

Don't do this, Rachel. Don't pull away from me.

I'm not. At least she didn't think she was.

You are. I can feel it in your silence.

The door to the sycamore room was now shut and the rest of the team had disappeared up the hall to the living room.

Duncan turned her toward him. "Talk to me."

The moment had blindsided her, reminding her that Duncan wasn't the only one with issues. She said softly, "What kind of life is this for anyone?"

He pulled her against him. "I don't know. Sometimes I wonder if I hadn't been the son of a famous Militia Warrior, I might have chosen a different path."

She was so stunned; she drew back and looked up at him. "You're serious? Duncan, I've never heard you so much as hint you would have ever done something else with your life."

"I know. And I also know, like you, I'm built for this life. It's a weird paradox."

She sighed. "There are moments, like this one, when the nature and sheer size of the mountain in front of us overwhelms me. Do you think those men in the vision were part of Merl's team?"

"I think it's even worse. I now believe Merl served as the leader of the Warriors of the Blood on Third and when he left, he thought he was saving them all, his sister included."

"Oh, God," she whispered. "And instead, Yolanthe imprisoned them."

"And soon, she'll kill them. We have to get them all out. I see that now. But I have no idea how we'll be able to get the job done."

She felt it as well, the future hurtling toward the team, demanding more from each than she could have ever imagined.

He added, "Since I'm having visions, my guess is Yolanthe has a Seer or possibly several working for her. She might already know about us. At the very least, she's seeking information about me. I know she's not finished trying to put me back in harness."

Rachel sighed and for a moment laid her head on his chest. The future felt so uncertain yet full of demands. She'd already made the commitment to the team, and she wouldn't back out now, but Merl's distress had definitely reminded her of all the stakes involved.

~ ~ ~

Duncan held Rachel close, not wanting to let her go.

There was nothing simple in this group of warriors. If what Duncan believed was true, Merl felt responsible that his men were in prison, God help him.

After a moment, he released Rachel. "We should join the others."

"I know."

82

Once in the living room, Jean-Pierre held up a box. "Rachel, this is for you. Warrior Santiago sent it over when I told him I would be seeing you tonight."

Rachel went to Jean-Pierre immediately, taking the box from him. "My new daggers. And he said he was having a holster set made as well."

"A holster set?" Jean-Pierre asked.

Rachel shrugged. "That's what he called it."

"Not a belt?" Duncan had no idea what Santiago had been up to.

"Nope." Rachel sat down and settled the large box on her lap. She flipped the latch and lifted the lid, then pulled out a black leather belt with two holsters attached and leather strings dangling from the end of each.

Holding it up, she said, "I get it now. These strings tie around my thighs. Genius." She glanced at Duncan. "Look, there are four angled slots on each side panel. I'll have ten daggers at my disposal, four on each hip and two in my weapons harness. This is perfect."

At the bottom of the box were eight daggers in a row, each in its own sheath.

She carefully took the first one out, her eyes wide. "He made these himself, didn't he?" She glanced up at Jean-Pierre.

"*Oui, bien sur.* He is a craftsman and he is obsessed."

Duncan knew Santiago had a love of weaponry, including daggers, and was always working on some new project or other. When he'd seen Rachel's skill a couple of weeks ago at HQ, he'd told her he'd put something together for her. Duncan had thought maybe he'd create a new blade. Instead, he'd made eight.

Rachel stood up and immediately donned the belt, using the strings to tie each holster down around her thighs. Duncan had to take a few deep breaths because the whole look got to him, leather on leather, each dagger sliding into its slot, and Rachel's eyes glittering.

"I can't wait to do some practicing." She palmed one of the daggers from her right holster. "Oh, yeah. This is fantastic."

Duncan had to look away. But Jean-Pierre caught his eye and grinned at him, a very knowing look that made Duncan shake his head.

"I think we are in need of some distraction, *non*?" He asked quietly. "How about that beer?"

Jean-Pierre laughed as he headed into the kitchen. "Follow me. I think after what Merl has just gone through, we could all use a break."

As Jean-Pierre handed Duncan some beers, he shouted a loud 'heads up' and began tossing them to the rest of the team. Each of the men caught a bottle and offered up a whoop of appreciation in response.

"Before you open them, take them onto the deck," Jean-Pierre called out. "If these floors see even a single drop of beer, Fiona will kick me from the bed and that I will not have, *mes frères*."

The men chuckled and headed outside.

Duncan drew near Rachel once more and handed her a beer, but she didn't take it. She glanced at the bottle and put a hand to her stomach. "I haven't eaten so this doesn't exactly appeal right now."

He narrowed his eyes. "But you always love a good beer, anytime."

"What I really want is some food."

"Jean-Pierre's housekeeper made a tray of sandwiches. He'll be bringing it out soon."

"Good, because suddenly I'm starved." Keeping warriors fed was a big part of the nightly routine and Rachel was one of them now.

"You like your new holsters?"

"Are you kidding? I love them."

Because the team was on the deck and Jean-Pierre was still in the kitchen, Duncan leaned close and whispered. "And I'm loving the look. Just sayin'."

Rachel shifted to telepathy. *You mean this leather tied around my thighs?*

84

Oh, yeah.

Rachel leaned up and kissed him, a lingering kiss that made him wish they were alone. When she drew back, she planted a hand on his weapons harness, and sent, *That's enough for now. Any more of this and I'll have to haul you into the woods.*

Duncan chuckled and shook his head. "You're right." He stepped away from her. *Though you might want to leave the holster set behind, at least for now.*

I think I'd better because you're shedding your spicy ale scent like there's no tomorrow and I'm about ready to crawl all over you.

When she reached between her legs to untie the leather strings, he had to turn his back to her. Of course, he caught sight of Jean-Pierre watching him and grinning all over again. But there was also compassion in the Frenchman's eyes, so Duncan wasn't annoyed.

Jean-Pierre knew the drill. Not so long ago, the *breh-hedden* had slammed down on his head in the shape of the former blood-slave, Fiona.

Once Rachel had settled the holster set back in the box, he led her out onto the deck and handed off the extra beer to Josh.

The moment the large platter of food appeared, the men began to devour and a lot of the tension dissipated. Rachel took a chicken salad sandwich and settled herself at the table. He watched her for a moment, concerned about her stomach troubles. Maybe the stress of battle had been getting to her more than she was willing to admit.

He picked up a roast beef sandwich on a thick bun and began his own devouring act.

A few minutes later, Owen sat down on a bench next to Luken. He dangled a beer between his legs with two fingers, and held a half-eaten sandwich in his free hand. "Maybe it's time we cut Merl loose."

Alex, who'd been ribbing Joshua about some event at the Blood and Bite involving two women and the red velvet booths, called out, "What the hell, Owen? The man just learned his team's been chained

85

up, probably for as long as he's been here. We don't need to cut him loose, we need to cut him some slack."

Luken, however, didn't jump on Owen, but asked, "Why did you say that?"

"Has it occurred to anyone else he might be feeding info to Yolanthe to keep his sister safe? Things about the black ops team? About Duncan?"

"*Merde*," Jean-Pierre murmured.

Joshua warmed to the theme. "He might have been holding back teaching us what we need to know to battle on Third." He now had two empty beer bottles lined up on the deck railing.

Because Josh's observation was a real possibility, a weight settled on the team.

A few weeks back, Duncan might have suggested the same thing as Owen — just get rid of the problem. He might even have had the same attitude two nights ago. But something had shifted inside him, and instead of reacting, he moved away from the group, turning to face the grove of sycamores. He directed his attention inward, toward his vision power. Energy hummed through his body. He closed his eyes, aware he was probably emitting a faint gold light from his skin.

He focused on Merl and on the men he'd seen in the vision. He wanted to know more before Merl returned in case a decision had to be made.

Trust was the real issue. Duncan had always felt uneasy about Merl and not just because he'd once flirted with Rachel. He'd been hostile during training and withdrawn everywhere else. All of which now made sense. But could the team trust him?

What arrived suddenly in vision form, wasn't a look into the future at all but well into Merl's past and was comprised of a montage of images. He saw Merl in front of large groups of Militia Warriors, his expression almost as intense as Owen's was right now. He was heavily involved in training Militia Warriors in many of the images, demonstrating battle skills, giving individual and group instruction on technique and strategy.

A few of the visions involved hundreds of warriors, all aligned against either Yolanthe or her father, Chustaffus.

Another set of images showed Merl, with his maroon leather battle harness and black kilt, doing battle with the same group of warriors Duncan had seen in Yolanthe's prison. The men made use of the *cadroen* but wore what Duncan could now see was a traditional set of three braids on either side of the face, though pulled back into the clasp as well.

In these images, Duncan's instincts were proved right since Merl always handed out the night's assignments; Merl was the team leader. But instead of sending the men to dimensional Borderlands, as Luken would have done on Second Earth, he sent them to various 'camps' around the world. Merl had been in charge of the resistance movement on Third Earth.

He had the answer he needed and the vision dissipated. When he turned around, the team was staring at him, a couple of mouths agape. Glancing at Rachel, she said quietly, "Your *grayle* power was rising from your body in at least three streams of bluish smoke."

He didn't address their obvious combined astonishment, but related what he'd just witnessed. As he finished up with Merl's leadership of the Third Earth Warriors of the Blood, he realized Merl now stood in the doorway, Endelle behind him.

He met the warrior's light blue eyes. "Did you get all of that?" Duncan asked.

Merl nodded. "Accurate as hell."

Duncan saw at once the warrior was changed. The revelations of the earlier vision of Yolanthe's prison had stripped Merl's façade away completely. He looked like a different man, more like the one in Duncan's vision, a leader and a warrior.

Merl moved across the deck, placing himself in the middle of the

CARIS ROANE

team. "You must have questions. As the Creator is my witness, I'll answer every single one of them."

Owen rose to his feet. "I have a big one. Have you been serving as Yolanthe's spy, telling her about us?"

"Not about the black ops team because she doesn't know what I've been up to. Although I suspect that's about to change. But yes, I reported information to her about Second Earth."

Endelle moved to stand beside Duncan.

Joshua rubbed the tats on his wrist and directed his hard brown eyes at Merl. "Why the fuck didn't you tell us what was going on? Why didn't you trust us?"

"How could I have done that? I was protecting Katlynn and at the same time trying not to get any of you killed. I have to deliver reports once a month as it is."

Owen entered the fray. "So, you're a spy, and what did you tell the bitch about Thorne's operations on Second? Holy fuck, you've seen everything."

Luken rose to his feet as well, but addressed Owen. "Dial it down, Warrior. Give him a chance to explain himself. And remember, Yolanthe as a Third ascender isn't going to be all that interested in things on Second. She'll consider herself superior because, well, she probably is. Any arrogance she might have will work for us."

The way Owen's nostrils flared suggested he was still gearing up for a shout down.

Luken once more intervened. "Before Merl says anything, let me tell you what I think happened, then Merl can tell me if I'm wrong. So here goes: Merl either fed Yolanthe a pack of believable lies or reported inconsequential data. You've seen him, the martinis and cigarettes. Samuel told me the first time he met Merl, he wore some kind of silk dressing gown. He's been playing this game for a long time and probably has Yolanthe suckered in."

88

Owen scowled at Luken, but as he turned to Merl, he asked, "Does Luken have it right?"

Merl nodded. "Yolanthe has a deviant nature, sexually I mean, so I fed her lots of details about my supposed exploits on Second. When she learned I'd gotten close to Endelle, I fabricated an entire history for her."

At that, he heard Endelle chuckle. "How much of a history?"

"Enough to keep her entertained and distracted. She seemed to enjoy my reports which I believe kept her from investigating further. And if it's of any use, for years she was mostly focused on Darian Greaves and his ambitions. I happily told her anything I saw on TV."

"Why did she give a fuck about Greaves?" Joshua swigged his third beer.

"She had a crush on him."

For some reason, these words lightened the moment and laughter traveled around the group. Only recently, Endelle had battled Greaves out at White Lake, and ended his world-encompassing campaign to take over Second Earth. Of course, the army he'd built had splintered into three factions each headed up by a general full of a similar type of ambition. Second Earth was in a worse state now that Greaves was gone. And there was strong indication Yolanthe's father, the powerful Chustaffus who'd enslaved two-thirds of Third Earth, was making a bid to rule Second as well.

Rachel entered the discussion. "What do you mean, Yolanthe's deviant side?"

Duncan turned to her and answered the question. "I told you about her sex pool."

"Sex pool?" Alex grinned. "This is getting interesting."

Another chuckle went round the group.

Duncan grimaced, however. Yolanthe had kept his attention focused on all her activities through her Third Earth voyeur window and it had not been pleasant. He decided to set the record straight.

"When you're forced to watch for hours on end, believe me a certain monotony follows. I couldn't shut her voyeur window down. And she used sex slaves, which enraged me since I couldn't do a damn thing for any of them."

He turned to Rachel. "I'm sorry about what happened, but I wanted you to know the truth."

She lifted her chin and her lips curved. She took his hand in hers. "Spoken like the man I know and love."

For several intense seconds, Duncan couldn't breathe. The way Rachel saw him was the man he wanted to be. "Rachel," he said softly.

"Oh, for Christ's sake," Endelle blurted. "The *breh-hedden* sucks donkey's ass."

Laughter traveled the circle of warriors. Even Merl smiled, a true smile, something he no doubt hadn't done in a long time.

Chapter Six

Freedom comes in a thousand different forms.

Collected Proverbs — **Beatrice of Fourth**

Endelle sat on the bottom row of the workout center risers at Apache Junction HQ. She'd changed into black leather pants because she kept flashing the warriors inadvertently in her red tulle skirt and small modesty slip. She didn't mind, not giving a damn who saw the beauty between her legs. But Owen took a skin burn across his abdomen when Josh got distracted.

She just wasn't much for keeping her knees together.

But she still wore the bejeweled dagger vest and her hip boots.

Her gaze drifted to Merl as she leaned her elbows back on the bench. The warrior had transformed into a dynamo so that between the efforts of Jean-Pierre who could enhance powers and Merl's new motivation, the team had finally started responding. Each showed evidence of the *grayle* power, a Third Earth ability having several ramifications. All the warriors had improved in faster wing-release as well as wing-retraction and quicker response with sword and dagger-work.

Duncan's vision had delivered a brutal blow to the one-time leader of the Third Earth Warriors of the Blood. Merl's secret about how he'd ended up on Second had finally come out. But after all was said and done, the result had put him on the right course.

Apparently, Yolanthe had kidnapped his sister, Katlynn, and used

91

her to send Merl to Second to serve as Yolanthe's spy. She'd even paid for his personal portal, the one in the wall of his living room, which the black ops team used to enter the darkening grid. But she'd held the threat of Katlynn's death over his head for fifty years.

What he hadn't known was that Yolanthe had afterward lured his What-Bee team into a trap, though Merl still didn't have a clue how she'd done it. Yolanthe's ability to somehow take control of so many extremely powerful Warriors of the Blood at the same time and hold them for five decades, spoke volumes for the woman's natural level of power.

Yolanthe's apparent obsession with Greaves made less sense than anything else Endelle had heard, but, *whatever*. Although the thought of Yolanthe and Greaves together sent a shard of fear wiggling her tailbone. Thank the Creator Greaves was locked up on Fourth. From Beatrice's last report, Endelle's former Nemesis was suffering acutely in Beatrice's redemption pools.

Endelle smiled. Imagine Greaves developing a conscience.

Merl called out a new drill and each of the warriors, including Rachel, lined up, knees bent, eyes forward. He was improving their wing-mounting speed. A lot of Third Earth powers seemed to be connected to the wing-locks, including the *grayle* power.

He called a three-count and on three, each of them released their wings at Third Earth speed and it was magnificent. She almost applauded. Only Owen was late, a full three-seconds after the others.

She considered Owen for a moment. Damn, but he was good-looking with his hazel eyes and a lick-able cleft chin. His hair was brown but with blond streaks like Jean-Pierre. The latter was with him now, a hand on his shoulder, feeding Owen his bump-up power surge to help bring his lagging abilities forward.

Owen scowled, however, and wouldn't look at Merl. The chemistry was really off between these two warriors in particular and nothing about the recent revelations had softened Owen's attitude. Endelle had asked him what bug was still reaming his ass, and had gotten a clear response, 'I can't respect a man who gets his team imprisoned. How can I trust him now?'

Endelle knew she could offer no words to alter Owen's opinion. Time would hopefully change things, but Merl had a lot of proving to do.

The next drill involved retracting their wings, but at the same time holding onto the wing-release power in order to jump-start the *grayle* abilities. Both Joshua and Alex had *grayle* smoke rising from their bodies and Merl gave a shout of triumph because of it. Joshua's had a violet hue and Alex's leaned toward silver.

Endelle shifted her gaze to Luken. He stood with eyes closed, concentrating fiercely. The next moment, a heavy stream of smoke emerged swirling from his wing-locks, three colors at once, all flowing together: gold, violet, and teal.

One-by-one, each of the warriors turned to stare.

A shiver traveled across Endelle's shoulders and down her spine. What was she looking at? She felt confused and amazed at the same time.

"Merl, what does this mean?" she called out.

Merl shook his head. "I don't know. I've never seen multi-colored smoke before."

Luken. Again. Another sign something extraordinary was going on with him.

Luken asked what they were talking about, then looked up and his eyes widened. "Sweet Jesus, what the hell is that? I don't get it. Why three colors?" He shifted his gaze to Merl.

Merl shrugged. "I don't know. Power, I would guess, perhaps to match your physical dimensions."

Alex added his two cents. "Tank-like smoke for a tank-like warrior."

Laughter rolled through the team.

But Endelle couldn't even smile. Instead, the familiar pressure inside her head increased suddenly as her gaze remained fixed on Luken. She rubbed her forehead. The damn headache hadn't let up and she'd even contacted Jeannie at Central to see if a storm was moving in to account for the persistent pain.

No storm, however, just one nagging headache, something she rarely experienced given her self-healing abilities. She even contemplated hauling Horace over to Militia HQ just to get some relief. But she hated bringing him in when he spent every night patching up those warriors engaged in battling at the Second Earth Borderlands. They fought death vampires dusk to dawn. So, she waited. But if the pressure didn't abate by daybreak, she'd call him to the palace once he was done for the night.

Duncan's vision had changed everything for the team, no question. And according to his time-table, they had a couple of nights to gain the necessary Third Earth abilities to battle anyone they encountered when they finally passed through Yolanthe's portal. But would these drills and so many emerging powers be enough? With the exception of Merl, the team simply wouldn't be seasoned in battle for the higher dimension.

The sound of Luken's voice, as he suggested repeating a drill, drew her attention back to the team leader. She'd never known a man like him in the course of her life, built like hell, stronger than everyone around him. When she'd first assigned him to take Thorne's place as leader of the Warriors of the Blood, she'd thought him a temporary replacement until she'd seen him in action.

Luken was a natural leader and had lived in Thorne's shadow. Now each man had a new job and if the Seers were right, Thorne would one day take her place as Supreme High Administrator of Second Earth.

But what about Luken? With so much talent and power, what was his destiny?

She repressed a sigh as her vision of a month ago once more rolled through her head of Luken sliced up during a battle on Third and falling from a point high in the sky all the way to earth.

The pressure in her head sharpened suddenly to the point of extreme pain. She rocked forward and held her head in her hands.

She realized she'd felt this before, as though something outside of her was trying to get inside her mind.

She sat upright and began to explore the crippling sensation. Then, instead of fighting the pain, she let it go.

And just like that, another vision rushed into her head. She levitated upward and felt as though she was falling backward at the same time.

She heard Luken shout her name.

The vision this time was of her, in a costume that rocked, lots of metal, horn and black leather, sort of a modern-day Viking, even better than the ones she'd sketched earlier.

Only where was she? The place was a deep woodland. She felt death vampires near her, maybe fifty yards out.

She turned, and there was Luken battling a large force of Third Earth Militia Warriors, sweating and struggling to keep up.

The next moment she had a sword in hand and she knew exactly what to do. She took up her place beside Luken and together they defeated the enemy.

The vision ended abruptly. She found herself staring up into the metal ceiling of the workout center and Luken was holding her in his arms. She turned into him, tears in her eyes as she put her hand on his face.

"Endelle?"

"I'm okay. You can put me down." She had trouble swallowing, though. Her throat was so tight.

"What happened?" he asked. "You were in the air, on your back, then dropping fast."

"You caught me?"

"Hell, yeah."

Endelle started laughing and couldn't seem to stop. "Well if this doesn't fuck me up one side and down the other."

The team had all stopped what they were doing and now surrounded them both.

Endelle looked from one face to the next. "I think my life just changed course and it looks like I have a new job."

But it was to Luken she turned and said, "You're not going to believe this, but I'm your goddam righteous Guardian of Ascension. You're ascending, Luken, that's what I know. You're leaving this dimension, moving on, and apparently – at least until that asshole Chustaffus is ground into a billion particles of burned up carbon – I'll be serving as your protector."

"What?" Luken looked like she'd just dumped a bucket of snails on his head.

"My sentiments exactly. And Merl, you're going to teach me how to access my *grayle* power so I can keep this man alive. For some reason, he has a big role to play in your dimension."

Silence reigned for a long moment, then the questions flew. What was the vision about? What had she seen? Why Luken? She answered them all, speaking at length about the details of the vision as well as what she felt in her heart.

When everyone's curiosity was satisfied and their concerns laid to rest, she contacted Thorne telepathically. She let him know he'd need to take over for her earlier than either had imagined.

The response he gave was to the point. *Tell me when and I'll take up residence in the palace.*

She chuckled to herself, then sent, *Let me guess. Marguerite has already given you a heads-up.* Thorne's *breh* was the most powerful Seer in all of Second Earth.

She did, early this morning. A slight pause, then, *Endelle, this is it, isn't it? You're moving on for good?*

Endelle's throat grew painfully tight. *Not sure, but it's feeling powerful to me. My only real concern right now is making sure Luken stays alive. Every long, curly hair on my head tells me neither of our dimensions will survive if he doesn't live to do battle with Chustaffus.*

Shit, I've got another group of Third Earth death vampires headed my way. I'll send Santiago to intercept. Chustaffus is making our lives hell here.

I know. We're on it from this end, but it's going to take time.

Wars always do. And Endelle, please stay in touch. You're important to me.

She felt his telepathy disconnect before she could respond, before she could assure him she would always make an effort where their relationship was concerned. Thorne was family to her.

Having settled things with him, Endelle turned herself over to Merl for training.

With just a few brief instructions, she had to admit she rocked the new Third Earth moves. Merl had been right; she'd taken about three minutes to excel at folding while in wing-mount, though the rest of the team still struggled. Her *grayle* power turned out to have an excellent scarlet stream of smoke and her abilities to wield a sword came roaring back.

It might have been a few centuries since she actually went into battle, but her muscle memory was as sharp as the tip of her blade.

As far as her powers went, the only area where she struggled was in levitating, something those ascenders from Third Earth and the Upper Dimensions could do easily.

While attempting to levitate and falling on her ass a few times, Merl finally took her aside and asked quietly, "What's going on? I would have thought levitation a cinch for you."

"Hell if I know. You're the teacher. What do you think?"

He narrowed his light blue eyes. Merl was a stubborn, handsome man and the recent revelation of having been the leader of the Third What-Bees before his exile only added to his good looks.

"I'll tell you what I'm sensing. You're holding back and that's not like you."

Endelle, not given to introspection, scowled as she stared in return. "I don't hold back." She ran her hand over her vest made up of thirty small, brass blades.

Merl smiled and for a moment seemed like the man she'd first met. He'd become so much more since his flirtatious period, but she'd missed this side of him. "I'm only suggesting that since this power eludes you, something has tripped you up. You regretting your announcement about being Luken's Guardian of Ascension?"

"No, not at all."

He glanced Luken's direction. "What is it about that man? I know he's a natural leader, someone you want to follow. But there's something more, something I can't put my finger on."

She turned toward Luken, whose blond hair had come loose from the *cadroen* and now flew about wildly as he worked on the latest folding-reappearing sword drill. He looked magnificent.

"He has a big-ass heart, like no one I've ever known. Maybe that's it. Even I feel safe when he's around." She chuckled. "And I'm supposed to be guarding him, but maybe that's why. I love him to death." Almost as much as she loved Thorne.

"Okay, but are you sure you're not regretting something?"

"Regret is the wrong word." She turned her attention back to Merl, meeting his gaze. "Well, damn my fine hips but I think I might be sad."

Merl's brows drew together. "Why?"

She shrugged. "I don't know. I've served as the ruler of Second Earth almost as long as I can remember. The Council of Sixth has kept me here to keep the peace on this planet and I haven't been allowed to ascend."

"I didn't know that. I guess I assumed you liked it here."

"It's never been about what I liked or didn't like. I've done my duty and I'm happy to have done it. But I've missed a lot." She gave herself a shake because she'd started sounding like a complainer. "I guess I never thought I'd actually leave Second Earth before the conflict was over."

"The battle with Greaves didn't end anything."

She shook her head. "Made things worse. Seems he wasn't the only ambitious asshole in his troops. And now there are three generals trying to take a bid for Second Earth, each getting Chustaffus's support. Thank God Thorne has charge of the military operation."

"But extending my service to Third has left me with a strong sense I might be leaving Second for good."

"You're talking about more than just guarding Luken."

"I guess I am. And no, I can't explain it, but I feel strangely grief-stricken." And that was exactly the right phrase. One part of her life was finally, after so many millennia, coming to an end and another was beginning. She'd just never imagined when she took this step it would be to serve as a Warrior of the Blood on Third as well as Luken's Guardian of Ascension.

Having confronted the issue, Endelle felt surprisingly liberated. She glanced down at her rockin' boots and let her *grayle* power flow, the force that fueled all the other Third Earth powers. She spread her arms wide and began to rise in the air, completely wing-less.

Her red smoke billowed now and she began to spin in place though at least four feet above the wood floor of the workout center. She stopped the spin and rose swiftly to the rafters, then dropped fifteen feet in a straight line. Afterward, she spun toward the entrance, holding her trajectory thirty feet above the floor.

Then she really let herself go.

She dove, tucked, and rolled.

She spun sideways, then stretched out horizontally and spun herself toward the rafters once more.

Freedom had come to her after thousands of years of service on Second and in a form that stunned her. She'd never known such exhilaration as doing a series of flips, twist and rolls through the air, all without her wings.

Below, the warriors had moved to the perimeter of the black workout mats and watched her. But she wasn't performing for them, only for herself.

A very pure kind of joy had replaced her grief, at least for the moment, and she allowed herself full expression.

~ ~ ~

Duncan crossed his arms over his chest as he watched She-Who-Would-Live flying through the air, not a wing in sight.

Unbelievable.

He couldn't help but smile. And whatever Merl had said to her had done the trick, removing Endelle's learning block.

Her sudden and complete shift to Third Earth warrior made him turn his attention for a moment to Rachel. Her change had been no less dramatic or thorough. She stood near Luken, her eyes wide as she watched Endelle maneuver, glide, and occasionally streak through the air.

His woman was a warrior now, something he'd thought she would never become. But the times had demanded a great deal of them both, and neither had arrived at a final destination. Duncan knew he had so much to learn and each of his Third Earth emerging powers would require months if not years to refine. Though he had taken on the role as the one who would define the team's missions from night-to-night, he knew in his heart his end-point on Third would be very different from his duties as a warrior.

Rachel was no different. She'd spoken earlier while at Jean-Pierre's about questioning her current warrior life. They were in most respects stuck in a middle ground of learning without truly knowing what the future would hold for each of them.

When Rachel turned toward him, she mouthed, 'Oh, my God,' then reverted her attention to Endelle.

He felt the same way, marveling at the woman who'd been stuck on Second for thousands of years.

Endelle only stopped her aerial theatrics when she paused to levitate upright in the air and drew her phone from her leathers. With her cell to her ear, she began a slow descent. Once she touched down, she turned in his direction and waved him over.

He crossed without hesitation.

How different everything seemed now that he'd launched his *grayle* power, because as he focused on Endelle, he felt a vision hover within his mind, waiting for his attention.

When he drew close, she shoved her phone back into her pocket, then said, "That was Thorne. He's got several of his men, including Warrior Santiago, pinned down by Third Earth death vampires. Looks like Chustaffus has started bumping up his game." He saw the concern in her wooded eyes as she planted a hand on his shoulder. "What have you got for me because if you can provide a vision, I can get them out of there right now."

Duncan let the vision roll and as it did, he knew Endelle could see it within her mind at the same time. He wasn't sure if it was his *grayle* power or hers, but whatever the case, sharing a vision saved a lot of time.

The vision basically showed the exact location of the besieged troops and the next moment, Endelle, within the vision, showed up in the outfit she currently wore, a sword blazing in each hand.

A plume of red smoke created a vaporous cloud around her as she struck at least a dozen of the bastards down. The swift sequence of her strikes made it impossible for any of the death vampires to even see her.

When the vision drew to a close and a cheer rang out from Santiago and the Militia Warriors on the ground, the vision dissipated.

Endelle dropped her hand away from his shoulder. "Excellent. And what intrigues me is how clear the time-frame is. I've got five minutes. Well, done, Duncan."

Instead of leaving immediately, however, she moved in Merl and Luken's direction. She quickly detailed the nature of the vision and what she'd be doing.

She didn't wait for either of the men to respond, she simply folded from the workout center.

Merl didn't let but a handful of seconds lapse before he called out to the team, "Listen up. I need all of you on the wing-mount fold. We don't stand a chance against either Third Militia Warriors or death vampires unless the team has mastered this skill."

~ ~ ~

Rachel followed after the men, her thoughts still caught on having watched Endelle perform an amazing series of levitating and tumbling moves. That Duncan then shared a battle vision with Endelle had left her feeling wired, but not in a bad way.

Yet what stuck in her head was the reality she was part of the whole thing, especially because of her Fourth Earth shielding power. She could mount her wings faster than ever before and she'd started releasing her own green *grayle* smoke as a result of these advances.

She vibrated with energy and power.

As Merl levitated and moved swiftly up and down the line, her gaze was fixed on him. He had an intensity now he'd not had before. She felt his determination and understood the cause since rescuing Katlynn, as well as the other warriors, bore heavily on each of their minds. Merl's ability to communicate to the warriors had improved immensely and each warrior was really responding to the combined efforts of Jean-Pierre and Merl.

He spoke about holding the *grayle* power tight as the wings released, so that the mounting of the wings fed into the *grayle* surge. Only with the two combined, wings and *grayle,* could the fold be accomplished.

Rachel closed her eyes and held out her hands, feeling her own *grayle* energy rise. She recalled Merl having slapped Duncan on the chest, saying the power came from the core of the body, the very soul. She let the power flow and when she felt the *grayle* connect with her wings, the increased vibration of energy let her know she could do the fold.

She didn't hesitate, but mounted her wings and the moment they released fully, she folded all the way to the entrance of the workout center, then materialized. There was no pain, no disrupted mesh super-structure, only a swirl of green smoke rising all around her.

It took her a moment to realize the men were all cheering her. She grinned so hard her cheeks hurt. She was one of them and the good Creator had given her an abundance of power so that she could serve on the ops team.

With the same confidence, she repeated the movement, arriving back at her starting point.

Merl drew close, his light blue eyes glowing. "Well done, ascender."

Backing up, Merl addressed the team. "Since Rachel is on fire, we're going to practice her shielding right now, along with some team signals I want all of you to learn. Because of the field we'll be attacking, I want Rachel capable of reaching the team at a distance of sixty feet. And don't worry, we'll get to each of your wing-mount folds in a bit."

Alex whistled. "Rachel, you think you can cover us at sixty feet?"

"I'll damn-well try."

Merl added. "And we need to be able to fold together as a unit, in any direction, on command."

Owen scowled. "How the hell are we going to do that?"

"Well, I'll tell you." Merl then gathered everyone around and spent the next half hour drilling the team on directional gestures used in the field to move as a body, especially given Rachel's shielding properties.

Once each had the signals down, Merl positioned Rachel at various points.

She thought it would be impossible to do as Merl suggested. But each time she accessed her *grayle* power and released her shield, she seemed to increase in distance and accuracy, as well as a feel for the group as a whole.

As soon as she had the team covered, Merl would set up a battle scenario then direct one of the warriors to take the lead. Rachel's primary job was to keep the team shielded no matter what happened.

There were several jumbles and mishaps, warriors running the wrong direction and colliding with each other.

When Joshua misread a signal, turned the wrong way and knocked her down, Merl stopped the drill. He then spent another fifteen minutes reviewing the hand gestures.

An hour later, the team moved seamlessly and Rachel was able to encompass the sixty feet Merl had insisted on.

Merl called a rest and she flopped onto the black mats, sweating profusely. Merl passed around bottles of water.

As she glanced from warrior to warrior, she couldn't believe what they'd accomplished in twenty-four hours. It wasn't so long ago, tensions had run high and none of them had been able to do a fold while in wing-mount.

Her thoughts ran to the woman in the veil, to Katlynn, knowing all this effort was geared toward her rescue. Rachel couldn't imagine what it had been like for her to be inside a jail cell for fifty years. She replayed Duncan's earlier vision through her mind of the warriors and the woman. An urgency was on her, yet she, too, could feel the mission wouldn't take place for another night yet. Of course, this wasn't a bad thing since they needed to learn all their Third Earth skills first.

But would the team get there in time?

"You look really worried." Duncan sat down beside her. He stretched out his long legs and leaned back, supporting himself with his palms behind him.

"Just thinking about Katlynn." She swigged her water. "Do we still have the same timing? When we need to be there?"

He nodded. "Yes. We'll engage sometime tomorrow night."

Rachel breathed a sigh of relief. "That's good, because I'm getting worn out. I know we're not done yet, but I'm going to need some serious rest before we head back into the Third grid."

He smiled at her, his expression softening. "You're not alone."

When Rachel turned to look at him, he shifted a little more in her direction.

Her lips curved, "We haven't been alone much tonight."

"No. We haven't." The timbre of his voice had deepened. He searched her eyes and she wasn't surprised when his spicy-ale scent began to rise all around her.

He leaned close and whispered against her check. "Shield us, just for a couple of minutes."

She knew what he wanted and didn't hesitate to let her power flow. She knew the moment the shield was complete and so did Duncan, because he simply eased her onto her back, rolled on top of her, then kissed her.

As his kiss deepened and his tongue drove into her mouth, she grabbed his thick, muscled shoulders. He then sucked at her throat greedily, and she moaned.

He drew back just enough to kiss her cheek, the line of her jaw, then drift down her neck. *I'm hungry, Rachel. I need you.*

I want to feed you, Duncan, but we shouldn't be doing this.

He drew back, a tender half-smile on his lips. "Everything's changing, isn't it?"

She smiled. "I can definitely feel you changing." She arched her hips against his growing erection.

He chuckled. "Yeah, we shouldn't be doing this. Don't know what I was thinking."

He slid off her and sat up.

When she joined him, she was about to release the shield but he grabbed her arm. "Just give me a sec."

She covered his hand and held his gaze. "Hope the training ends soon."

"Me, too."

When he finally rose to his feet, she knew the stolen moment was over. She hopped up as well and at the same time, released her shield.

Merl called out. "You two having fun?"

Chapter Seven

New skills thrive, when the past is brought to heel.
Collected Proverbs – **Beatrice of Fourth**

Not even Merl's comment could touch Duncan's feel-good. The team had really started coming together, his visions were back, and for the most part the damn snake stayed quiet. It seemed the more he moved forward, the less the poison got to him.

Merl got the team going again. "Let's pick up with folding during wing-mount. Who wants to go first?"

"I do," Duncan said.

Merl nodded then moved to stand in front of him. He put his hand on Duncan's harness, over his heart. "Feel your *grayle* power here and when you do, access the energy of your wings at the same time, but don't release right away. You want a combined sensation, both abilities forging in sync. Without it, you'll end up with a mangle of wings that will take hours to heal." Jean-Pierre drew close as well and planted his hand on Duncan's shoulder, adding his jump-start stream of energy to the mix.

Duncan's entire body vibrated with renewed energy. He closed his eyes and focused on the interior of his being, on all he was as a Warrior of the Blood and as a man capable of delivering battle visions. His wing-locks were already swollen, ready for release. But as suggested, he held the sensation at bay, waiting.

He sustained his concentration until he could feel his *grayle* power flowing through his chest and his veins. It felt similar to his vision ability but centered on his wings this time.

"That's it," he heard Merl say. "You've got it."

Duncan opened his eyes and met Merl's gaze. Merl stepped away from him. "Don't think. Just mount and do the fold."

While holding his *grayle* power steady, Duncan mounted his wings, the sensation so reminiscent of sex that for a few seconds his body flooded with the same intoxicating hormones. The next moment, he slipped into nether-space, his wings fully intact.

He was surprised to find he could see everyone clearly, something that didn't happen during a normal fold. Still within nether-space, he moved down the line of warriors and experienced a profound connection to each, especially his former squad. He could sense their positions and their general emotional shape; Owen's intensity, Alex's positive nature, Joshua's determination.

He aimed for the same location Rachel had chosen and re-materialized at the entrance to the workout center. The line of warriors cheered, just as they had for Rachel. Alex threw a fist into the air and whooped a few times.

Slipping back into nether-space with barely a thought, Duncan reversed direction. This time, he rematerialized behind Merl and caught him in a symbolic chokehold, releasing him quickly afterward.

"And here's the beauty of this kind of fold," Merl called out. "You can see where you're going, which will be a huge factor during battle since not all Third ascenders can fold during wing-mount."

His eyes shining with battle fervor, Merl turned toward Duncan and gripped his shoulder hard. "You've got it."

Merl then directed him to teach Owen. "Show the brother how it's done."

The command to have Duncan work with Owen made sense in terms of team-building. And maybe there was a small part of Merl not wanting to get too close to Owen. Of all the warriors, Owen had expressed his dislike of Merl the most.

A lot had changed in the past few hours, but one night's behavior didn't automatically translate into trust.

Duncan retracted his wings as he crossed to Owen. The brother's hazel eyes glowed fiercely, matching Duncan's current temper. Each of them wanted to be ready to take on whatever Third Earth warriors they would meet in Yolanthe's prison.

Duncan centered his hand on Owen's battle harness, over his chest. "Feel the power here and begin accessing your wing-mount energy at the same time. Both powers need to merge *before* you release your wings. Once I released mine, I had the sense it was permanent and wouldn't unravel during the fold. But you'll know what I mean when it happens."

Owen narrowed his eyes, fixing his gaze at a point beyond Duncan. Because Duncan had taken Merl's position as teacher, he now felt what Merl must have felt when he had his hand on Duncan's harness. A vibration began to build beneath Duncan's palm, a steady rise of power.

"Holy shit," Owen said, his voice hushed, awed. "I can feel the *grayle* power rising."

"I know."

Duncan even knew the moment the two powers locked together within Owen.

The next moment, Owen released his wings, which had grey, brown, and blue bands on a black background.

When Duncan removed his hand, Owen vanished into nether-space. He turned around and, though he couldn't see Owen, Duncan could feel him moving around the entire perimeter of the workout center. He knew exactly where he was though he wasn't certain why.

He felt him stop behind Joshua, and wasn't surprised when he suddenly materialized then tapped Joshua on the shoulder.

Josh turned around Owen, startled. "Unbelievable."

Duncan shifted in Merl's direction. "I could sense where he was. Is that normal?"

Merl dipped his chin. "Because you've been through the process and you've served together as warriors, you'll be able to sense him, the others as well, you'll see."

To Owen, Merl said, "Normally, I'd have each of you take a turn showing another warrior, but I want Duncan to do it. Because of his extraordinary battle visions, he'll be the hub of our team probably for as long as we're together. You'll each want a strong connection to him since I suspect it won't be long before he can share his visions with us, maybe even simultaneously."

Merl turned back to Duncan. "Now get Joshua on board."

Over the next few minutes, Duncan went down the line and worked with Josh, Alex, and Luken. Each time, Jean-Pierre assisted with his usual power boost, though he admitted he knew the *grayle* ability wasn't in his wheelhouse yet. It was clear to Duncan the black ops team had special parameters that even so powerful a warrior as Jean-Pierre couldn't cross. The team was meant for Third and Jean-Pierre would stay behind to continue building the powers of the Militia Warriors on Second.

By the time the entire team had performed what had been an impossible move only a night earlier, the hour was late and dawn wasn't far away. Luken suggested they retire to the black Ops Cave.

Duncan held Rachel's hand as together they walked in the direction of the team's private rec center. His body hummed with renewed energy. He couldn't remember feeling this ramped up in a long time.

Part of him wanted to take Rachel straight home. The brief time alone with her while she shielded him had made up his mind; he'd share her bed from now on.

But as much as he was ready to get busy with her, another part of him knew the importance of taking a half hour or so with the team to shake off the night's adrenaline.

He went straight to the bar and started to mix Rachel a Vodka tonic, one of her favorite drinks, but she caught his arm. "I only want water. Lately, I just haven't been able to handle much else."

He frowned at her. "Are you sure you're okay?"

She lowered her voice. "I think I'm just not used to all the training and battling. I've also been nauseous off and on for a couple of weeks. I know it'll pass once I've adjusted."

"Water, then?"

"That would be great."

As he put ice in a tumbler and filled up the glass from a New Zealand bottle, he looked her over. The skin below her eyes had a faint bluish tinge, but otherwise she looked really good, healthy.

She'd been through an awful lot and he hadn't made things easier for her at all. But they were together now, and he could work at doing his part. "Here ya go."

"Thanks."

He poured himself a Bourbon County Stout. As soon as Luken had commandeered the space, he'd had a few cases imported from Mortal Earth. He joined Rachel at the table in the corner, sat down and began the process of letting the night go. It was hard to do, knowing Katlynn and Merl's What-Bee team were imprisoned. None of them were far from his thoughts and even now, the vision once more played through his head of seeing the men chained up and the woman controlled with the lavender veil.

He'd been under the thumb of their captor, which tended to increase his need to set them all free. Yet, he could feel within his soul the time wasn't right. The future had to play out in a specific way in order for his visions to be of use.

"Hey," Rachel said, extending her hand across the table. "What's set your jaw to grinding?"

Taking her hand, he hesitated telling her. But as he saw the concern in her lovely, blue eyes, he recalled his promise to make an effort. "Yolanthe's prisoners."

A faint smile curved her lips. "I've been thinking about them as well, and I can't wait to head into the Third grid and get this job done."

"Me, too. For now, though, it's tough to stop the tape playing over and over in my head."

"Finish your beer, because I can think of at least one way to distract you." She lowered her voice. "You game?"

Catching the direction of her thoughts, his heartrate soared. "Hell, yeah, I'm game."

~ ~ ~

Rachel stared into green eyes. Every part of her being vibrated with sudden need. In many ways, the *breh-hedden* drove her absolutely crazy. But right now, looking at Duncan, she thought the myth-that-wasn't-a-myth held a central core of absolute genius.

She'd always lusted after his beautiful, warrior body. Now, she craved him with a desire so intense she only wondered why she didn't faint when she looked at him.

His nostrils flared and his eyes might have rolled back in his head. She understood. The sharing of scents was a profound aphrodisiac and the more she thought about taking him to bed, the more scent she knew she had to be releasing.

Duncan's own response returned with a heavy hit of erotic spiced ale. The scent swirled through her brain, tapping every pleasure center possible.

He gulped down the remainder of his beer and rose from his seat, extending his hand to her. She took it and jumped up a little too quickly. She bumped the table with her thigh and almost knocked over his now empty beer bottle.

He smiled, a knowing smile, full of wickedness. His viper-demon appeared to be quiet, thank the Creator.

Rachel said good-night to the rest of the team and worked hard to keep a blush from covering her cheeks. With her fair skin, she could turn bright red in a split-second.

Duncan, however, wore a pleased smile, his head high.

Men and sex, always something of a competition.

Once at the landing platforms in the large hangar, he slipped into her head telepathically. *I have a surprise for you.*

You do?

I do. But it means we won't be going back to Paradise Valley.

Really? Where are we going then? She had a naughty thought. *You know, the White Lake Resort Complex has a couple of really kinky hotels.*

He chuckled as he led her to stand next to him on the platform. She held tight to his arm, loving the closeness.

I like the idea, he said. *I really do. But I still think you're going to like mine even better.*

She smiled, squeezing his arm. *The truth is, I don't care where we go. I just need you something awful. So where are we headed?*

He looked down at her. *About nine months ago, I bought a cabin not far from the Mogollon Rim, a few miles from Sedona.*

Her heart lit up. *You have a cabin? In the mountains?*

I do. It's near a stream and I dammed it up enough to make a pool for swimming. How does that sound?

She did a full body shiver as she thought about being in the water with Duncan. *Like heaven.*

When the officer in charge of the landing platforms signaled for them to leave, Duncan folded them both. She felt a swift glide through nether-space, afterward arriving in front of a large home set in the ponderosa pines of northern Arizona Two.

Not exactly a cabin, but quite beautiful.

At least thirty stone steps led at various angles up to a glass and timber house. "This is yours?"

"I bought it shortly after I had my first battle vision. At that time in my life, with new powers showing up, I thought I could use a retreat." He turned toward her slightly, pulling her into his arms. "But I think I may have bought this house because of you, Rachel, because I know how connected you are to nature."

She'd never been more surprised. "You did?"

"You always told me I was wound too tight. And I was. I am. I live with a constant sense of everything I do not being good enough. When I had my first vision and it unfolded in such a way lives were saved, I wanted something for myself, a reminder I'd done some good."

She smiled up at him. "You don't know who you are or how much good you've done every night of your warrior life. I hate your father for having torn away your self-belief from the time you were little."

"He was a bastard."

Rachel cocked her head. "I'm not sure you've ever said anything so true about Carlyon. Maybe he was a great warrior in the field, but he was a sadistic brute to his family."

Rachel recalled the tale Endelle had told of how Carlyon had chained Duncan in a basement when death vampires had surrounded his Militia Warrior force. Carlyon and his men had died that night, including Rachel's ex-husband, Grieg. And Duncan had only survived because he'd called for back-up. Luken had arrived just in time to beat back the deadly force.

A pained frown rode between his brows. "I never wanted to hurt you, Rachel. Never."

"But there were two of us in this relationship, Duncan. I've just started to recognize how every time you withdrew, I'd pull back as well. I'm trying hard not to react to you the way I used to."

He ran a hand down her back. "And I hate that your husband hurt you."

"Me, too. But it was the same tone your father set for his squad. I hope the Creator has the same baptismal pools Beatrice has on Fourth Earth. Carlyon should have to suffer in them because I'm told the perpetrator, once immersed in the pools, feels all the pain he's caused during his lifetime. Or hers, given the gender."

"You know, that would be a fitting punishment." He shifted his gaze away from her and an odd light came into his eye as he said quietly, "You know, I never knew what happened to my mother."

The shift to a parent he rarely mentioned, surprised Rachel. "What do you mean?"

"After my mother left, I never made an effort to find her, to learn her side of things."

"Why not? By the time you were an adult, you must have known she wouldn't have left unless she'd believed it necessary for her own safety, possibly even for yours."

"It's funny you would say that, because she said almost the same words to me when she left Carlyon's house. But you have to understand, my father filled me with his own propaganda, telling me she never wanted me. Despite knowing he'd lied, I still have so much rage when I think about her. She abandoned a child. How can that ever be forgivable?"

Rachel searched his eyes. "What exactly did she say when she left?"

"She said she was leaving so I'd survive."

Rachel wasn't sure how to say what she felt needed to be explained, but she tried anyway. "When a man has taken to hitting a woman, threatening her life day in and day out, he also uses any psychological tool at his disposal to strengthen his power over her. You and your safety, even your life, would have been a favorite pawn in his constant game of control and abuse of your mother."

The pain in his eyes deepened. He'd never talked so openly before and she could tell the wounds still hurt. "I know you're right," he said. "But he'd fed me on the poison of how weak she was, how cowardly, that I'd come to believe him. It's hard now to think otherwise."

"Duncan, her story is probably a very different one. You should find her if you can and really listen to her side of the tale."

"I've never wanted to." He glanced around suddenly as though the environs surprised him. "Well, how the hell did we get on this subject?"

Rachel knew not to push, so she said, "Why don't you show me your 'cabin'?" She did air quotes.

He smiled as he slid his arm around her waist and led her up the steps.

The downstairs was a huge vaulted space, leading to a typical 'A' shape for snowy climates. A massive stone fireplace graced the west wall and opposite at the far end was a large kitchen with an island.

Rachel felt dizzy suddenly and without warning wavy lines moved in front of her eyes, then an image appeared in the kitchen. She blinked several times because sitting on a stool at the island was a dark-haired little girl. Duncan was pulling a box out of the cupboard smiling at the child over his shoulder. "You want snails and bugs for breakfast, right?"

"Pancakes, Dad. I want pancakes."

His eyes twinkled as he set the mix on the counter in front of a large clear bowl. "Pancakes. Right. My mistake."

The girl giggled.

The wavy lines dissipated as quickly as they'd come. She knew she'd just looked into the future, that she'd had a vision of Duncan and his child.

The dizziness remained, however, and the next moment, her world turned black.

"Rachel. Rachel."

She heard Duncan's voice from far away. Her eyes fluttered open and it took her a moment to realize he was holding her in his arms. She was still very dizzy.

"Are you okay?" he asked.

She took deep breaths. "I saw something. At least I think I did." Or maybe she'd only seen what she wanted to see. Duncan had a little girl and she was her mother. Somehow, they'd become a family.

But the images, whether prophetic or not, struck a chord deep within her. She'd never thought she'd have children. Her marriage had proved fruitless, something she'd thanked God for repeatedly, and so had her on-again, off-again relationship with Duncan. They'd never used protection and she'd simply come to believe she was barren.

But was it possible she would one day have a child with Duncan?

For reasons she couldn't explain, the idea of it made her incredibly sad, because it seemed impossible on so many levels. She was a warrior now and Duncan had this viper in his gut. She had no confidence at all their current warm relationship would last.

"You can put me down now. I'm not dizzy anymore."

"Rachel, what the hell happened?" He set her on her feet, and she felt normal again.

"As I said, I think it might have been sort of a vision, yet not."

"What was it about? Yolanthe? The prisoners?"

She put a hand to her chest. "No, nothing like that."

"Then what? Tell me. I can feel how upset you are."

She stared at Duncan, her lips parted. "Would it be okay if I held onto this for a little while? The vision wasn't bad and it wasn't about the war on Third. But it's thrown me and I need some time to process, if that's okay."

She rubbed her hand over the top of his battle harness. "And I'm not pulling away from you, I promise."

He searched her eyes for a long moment. "Whatever you need to do is okay by me, so long as you're not in danger."

She shook her head. "No. Not at all."

Though her heart was, maybe. When she'd first been with Duncan ages ago, she'd wanted a family with him. But that was a long time past, so many fights in-between, so much impossible baggage to overcome.

"Now, how about you show me your bathing pool."

"You still want to go?"

And just like that, she shed the effects of the vision and the conversation about Carlyon. "I'm right here with you, and the only thing I want is a swim without a stitch of clothes on and everything else that follows."

His shoulders released their ready-to-attack mode and a half-smile curved his lips. "Then let's go."

With his arm around her, she felt herself glide back into nether-space as Duncan folded her to a nearby forest stream.

The pool was quite large and flowed from a shallow waterfall at one end to a manmade dam at the other. Nothing looked more inviting than diving into the dark water with dawn just lighting the sky in the east.

~ ~ ~

Duncan had no idea what Rachel had seen before she fell unconscious, or why she'd fainted after having the vision.

But he was worried about her. Maybe the battling and all their new Third Earth powers had taken a toll more than either of them realized.

She seemed to have recovered her balance both physically and emotionally. But between her nausea, her complete rejection of alcohol, and now a vision, his concern had ramped up. Rachel was an important person in his life. She had been from the time he'd first hooked up with her. And recent events had brought them even closer. The thought something could be physically wrong drove deep into his heart and set the serpent moving swiftly through his gut once more.

Don't leave me. The words left his mind too fast for him to call them back.

Rachel had just folded off her battle suit when she turned to him, her milky skin glowing in the soft moonlight. "Duncan, I'm not going to leave you. Is that what has your brow fixed in a tight line? I would never leave you."

She looked almost appalled that he'd think such a thing.

"I didn't mean to say that. I'm not even sure why I did. But I want you to be safe. And whatever it was you saw—"

She went to him and grabbed his arms with both hands. "The vision had nothing to do with the war, I promise you. It was something personal, something I've had on my mind for a long time. In some ways, it was very sweet, the images I mean."

"Nothing about doing battle? Or about training?"

"Not even a little bit. Now let it go, please, because I'm going to swim."

She turned away and stepped quickly into the water. As soon as she was waist deep she dove under and came up smiling. "This is exactly what I needed."

Duncan let his doubts and fears recede and with a wave of his hand, sent his battle suit to his Paradise Valley home hamper.

"Walk slow," she called out, treading water.

"Why?"

When her gaze fell to his cock, he laughed, then slowed his pace so she could have a good look. Even the water now carried her beautiful garden scent and he began to grow firm.

As he moved into the water, she paddled slowly in his direction. He'd always felt this way with Rachel, driven toward her. The *breh-hedden* had only intensified his need and desire for her.

When he was knee deep, he stopped. He held his cock in his hand as she closed the distance between them. She'd always loved this masculine part of his body. He took a few more steps until the fingertips of his free hand touched the water.

He held himself ready for her, knowing what he wanted her to do and what she'd always enjoyed doing.

As she drew close to his groin, her lips parted and his cock slid inside her warm, moist mouth. She latched on and began to suck, her hands grabbing his ass and squeezing hard. He closed his eyes, his hips arching, his cock sliding deeper into her mouth.

He moaned, pulled his cock back to the edge of her lips, then pushed in once more.

The motion had her nails digging into his flesh.

Shield us, he sent softly through her mind.

Without hesitation, he felt her vibration flow over him until he knew they were cloaked and safe. If the enemy, in any form, should show up, Rachel would be safe.

He dropped his hand to cup the back of her neck and rocked his hips faster. She groaned and he loved how responsive she'd always been to him. When he reached a point where it would be hard to hold back, he eased from her mouth. Dropping in front of her, he gathered her in his arms, then turned to float her in the water.

He took her out into the deepest part of the pool and spun her several times. She draped her arms and legs straight out, enjoying the ride. She giggled and the sound eased his heart. He'd missed this so much, missed the joy she'd always brought to his warrior life.

After a few spins, she wiggled out of his grasp, turned, then leaped on his chest. She flung her arms around his neck and kissed him, dipping inside his mouth when he parted his lips.

He held her tight against him as her tongue worked his mouth, teasing and pleasuring him.

I want to take you in the air, he sent.

She gasped and drew back to hold his gaze. "High in the air?"

He nodded.

"We've never done that before." He could see the glitter in her eyes and knew she was intrigued.

"I know. But ever since we started mounting our wings at Third Earth levels, I've wanted to extend the experience. You game?"

She smiled and pulled away from him, heading toward the rocky edge of the pool. Wings could handle water, but made movement much harder.

Once she was on the bank, he watched her close her eyes, hold out her hands palms up, and take several deep breaths. He could tell she was savoring the moment. Coupled with sex, wing-mount was incredibly erotic. She arched her neck and her nipples grew peaked as her wings suddenly exploded into the air.

Since becoming a Warrior of the Blood, Rachel's wings had grown in width and height. They were a shimmering pale green with dark brown bands. She wafted them slowly and rose a few feet into the air.

Her lips parted as she opened her eyes and met his gaze. She crooked her finger at him several times and smiled.

He left the water and moved to stand close to her. The height she'd risen allowed him to caress her from her narrow waist, down her curved hips and thighs, all the way to her feet. Wings offered all sorts of possibilities and this was one of them. Without bending his knees, he could kiss her navel. Then, as he began to move lower, she rose just high enough in the air so he could tend to her sex.

I like the way you're thinking, he sent.

And I love your tongue.

He took the hint, dipped between her folds, and began to lick. She moaned softly, her hips arching into his face.

He slid his arms around her hips and pressed her close. He kissed and licked her then took as much of her in his mouth as he could. She gave a small cry when he began to suck.

Her hands found the top of his head, her fingers driving through his thick hair.

Put your legs over my shoulders. Can you do that?

Absolutely. Rachel had always been willing to try new things.

He held onto her hips as she settled her legs on his shoulders. Fanning her wings slightly, she held herself in position and at the same time created a slight breeze flowing around them both.

When he tilted her backward just enough, the angle gave him access to her well. He rimmed her sex with his tongue then drove deep. He felt her back arch and her thighs grip him hard. He wanted to make her come in this position. He thrust faster and faster so that soon she was releasing a series of passionate cries.

I'm close, Duncan. Give it to me.

He sped up, moving vampire fast. Her body grew rigid and she cried out as her well spasmed with pleasure. He didn't stop thrusting with his tongue until she at last relaxed against him and slid her thighs from around his shoulders.

He pulled her down to him and embraced her by slipping his arms around her neck. Her wings wafted as she moved in close and pressed her hips against his.

I love you, Rachel. I love you so much. He kissed her deeply.

He felt her sigh against him. *You've always known how to work my body. Thank you.* She often expressed gratitude when he pleasured her, one more thing he loved about her.

He ground his hips against hers, letting her feel his arousal. Bringing her to a climax always made him hard.

She pulled away just enough to caress his face with her hands. Her wings moved softly through the air, though not enough to lift her off the ground.

"I love doing this with you, Duncan. I always have. I think it's my most favorite thing."

"Even more than working in your garden?"

She smiled. "Yes. As much as I love growing things," she reached low and palmed his thick talk, "I love growing this even more."

She pleased him, the way she talked, the way she savored his maleness, the way she held him higher than her favorite pastime. The viper within his gut lifted it's headed and showed its fangs. *How can she think so much of you? She doesn't know you. Not really.*

Duncan shut the reptile down and focused his attention on Rachel. "I'm going to mount my wings now."

~ ~ ~

"Do you want to come while you mount?" There was so much

pleasure with wing-release, adding an orgasm would be an amazing experience.

She'd never done this with him before, though. She didn't exactly wait for an answer as she lowered herself just enough to take him in her mouth and suckle him. After a minute of enjoying his cock and hearing him moan, she slowly stood upright, took his cock in hand, and used the moisture to work him.

His lips parted and he was breathing hard through his mouth. "Do you want me to come like this?"

A slow-smile overspread her lips. "I only suggest it because lately you've been able to come more than once when we've been together. Why not now at the same moment you release your wings? Have you ever done this before?"

He smiled at her. "Only alone and in private."

Her eyes widened. "Then let me do it for you while you mount."

He nodded. "I'd love it."

She drew close to him and began stroking him, her other hand sliding around his waist. He planted both hands on her hips to keep her in place. He began breathing hard, panting against her cheek. "Rachel. Oh, God, that feels incredible."

She slid one hand over his wing-locks. As swollen as they were, they streamed moisture. She glided her fingers over the sensitive apertures through which the wings would release. He arched and cried out. "Oh, shit, that feels good. Keep doing that. I'm close."

She stroked his cock faster and kept rubbing his lower wing-locks. She could feel his wings ready to mount, so she moved her hand away and focused all her attention on his erection.

She slipped inside his head, *Come for me, Duncan. Come now. Yes.*

The moment he began to release his wings, he cried out and his cock began to jerk in her hand. She kept a steady, quick tug of her fist on his stalk, loving the shouts that erupted from his throat as his wings unfurled.

He let out a roar as he came, his warm seed spreading over her abdomen.

When his body settled down, and the tips of her wings batted against his, she let go of his cock. He leaned his forehead against hers. "That was fantastic."

"Next time, you can do the same for me."

He drew back enough to meet her gaze. "With pleasure."

After a moment, she backed away and turned to wade into the stream. She rinsed off his semen, then returned to him.

But when she glanced down at his groin, she gasped. "You're still hard."

His eyes were at half-mast. "I'm liking this rise in powers. It's helping other things stay where they ought to stay."

His spicy ale scent flowed over her in heavy waves, teasing her sex and causing her legs to tremble. She swept her wings forward then back just enough to lift her up then catapult herself into his arms.

He caught her around the waist, and with a brisk downward sweep of his wings, he took her into the air. He moved swiftly so that within seconds they were out of the forest and flying up toward the stars.

She kept her shield tight, knowing death vampires could be anywhere and who knew when Yolanthe would decide to show up.

Eventually, he slowed and with a gentle flapping of his wings sustained them midair. "Why don't you bring in your wings and let me do the work." He kissed her neck, suckling above the vein.

I'd like that.

As soon as Duncan drew back and took her hands in his, she focused on her wing-locks. With a few deep breaths and her new Third ability, she brought in her wings with one swift, unbelievable thought.

"It's amazing, isn't it, the way the *grayle* power has of enhancing everything?"

"Incredible." He was careful how he moved her close, always keeping one hand on her. She wasn't able to levitate, so without her wings she'd fall.

But Duncan, as a warrior, was a very physical man, his body honed, his reflexes sharp. She felt very secure with him.

With one arm draped over her back and his hand on her ass, he said, "Wrap your legs around my waist."

The sheer strength of his muscled arms, helped draw her entire body against him, even helping her pelvis to arch.

With her legs secured around his waist, she locked them in place.

He stared into her eyes, his wings wafting slowly overhead. "Use your hand and guide me in." His smile was seductive.

She reached between their bodies, and once more held his cock in her hand. Tilting her pelvis, she guided him to her well. The moment he entered her wetness, she moaned. Nothing felt better to her than this intimate connection.

He held her tight against him and with his wings moving in a slight backward stroke, he began to drive into her.

She clutched his arms, savoring the feel of him. The sight of the stars appearing and reappearing with the rhythmic movements of his wings, brought her heart swelling. The moment felt so full and nothing pleased her soul more than being under the heavens, in the air, secure in Duncan's arms while he made love to her.

Love was what she felt, all her affection for him, and her desire. *Feed from me Duncan. Take my blood.*

He moaned as she angled her throat for him. Even while his wings wafted in the air, his strike was true. He formed a seal around the wound and began to suck.

The *breh-hedden* came to life in a new way in that moment. She began to see what it would be like to bond with him, to experience a permanent deep connection to him.

If they ever completed the mate-bonding, she would be able to

125

feel what he felt at any given moment and he could know her physical location and her activities. Nothing would be more intimate.

She let herself enjoy these thoughts as he drank from her and rocked into her. His hips moved faster now, her pleasure rising as she flew toward the pinnacle of release.

Duncan, she sent, tears in her eyes, desire building in a heavy sensation deep between her legs.

Rachel. His voice pierced her mind, adding to all the sensations.

He groaned heavily as he used the momentum of the wings to push into her with his hips. He drove faster and harder.

He left her neck, which meant he was close.

A soft cry slipped past her lips as she met his gaze. Her breaths came in small gasps, until suddenly the orgasm barreled down on her, catching her tight between her legs with each thrust of his cock. She screamed, pleasure pouring through, gripping her low, and filling her chest with an incredible explosion of ecstasy. Duncan thrust faster than ever and finally began his second release.

His roars pressed against her screams as the orgasm spun through her mind. On and on, ecstasy spiraled through her body, flooding her veins with pleasure, and sending her straight into the heavens.

After a full minute of so much sweet sensation, the movement of his hips slowed. The sensual feel-good eased through her veins and caused her legs to finally grow lax.

Duncan shifted them to a more upright position and let his wings shape into parachute mount, rocking them both in place. With her arms now around his neck she kissed him over and over, thanking him for the extraordinary moment.

On the way down, she rested her head against his shoulder, trusting him completely. But the fatigue of the night's training settled on her and before he touched down outside the mountain home, she'd drifted off.

She awoke only when he was putting her to bed. As Duncan headed into the shower, she realized her nausea had returned, which seemed really strange. She began to wonder if she'd contracted some kind of stomach ailment that shouldn't really exist on Second Earth. Or maybe it was just a result of the intensive training she'd received.

Whatever the case, she decided she'd seek out a healer's advice the next night when she returned to HQ. She might even contact Horace whose team tended to the wounds of those who served as either Militia Warriors or a What-Bees.

With the decision made, she fell sound asleep.

Chapter Eight

The team soars,

When human nature settles its wings.

Collected Proverbs – **Beatrice of Fourth**

Duncan awoke before Rachel late in the afternoon. He made a pot of coffee and took a mug out onto the east-facing porch. The sun was well on its way to setting, so he had a clear view of a granite out-cropping, several forested ridges, and a lot of deep blue sky.

Rachel. Sweet Christ, making love with her high in the air had been an amazing experience. He'd never felt so connected to her. He'd been swept into a different reality, one that pointed him toward Third Earth. Yes, he'd serve on the black ops team as long as he was needed. But he also felt a strong call to something else, something more, though he had no idea what. And Rachel was part of it.

He accessed his *grayle* power and focused for a moment on the veiled woman the entire team now believed was Merl's sister, Katlynn. He also held the Third Earth Warriors of the Blood in his mind. Images arrived swiftly of a quiet prison setting, holding steady, and he could breathe easily. He knew for the moment all was well.

But the earlier vision lived in him at the same time, pressing him to stay tight and focused. The hour would come and the black ops team would head for Mexico City Three through the Third Earth darkening grid.

He felt different within himself and with Rachel, stronger. He'd reached a new level of power, as they all had, but he'd also begun staring down the serpent in his gut. He didn't know how he would make the *breh-hedden* work, but he was more committed than ever before.

He was still concerned about Rachel and her stomach sickness. She didn't seem like herself. She'd resisted becoming a warrior for so long, maybe it was all too much. Yet, he knew she was committed to serving on the team.

He'd just have to keep an eye on her.

~ ~ ~

Lying on her stomach, Rachel took her time waking up. She felt almost dazed and when she opened her eyes, her surroundings didn't look familiar. Then she remembered Duncan had brought her to his mountain home.

She blinked and took a deep breath, forcing the veil of sleep away. Fatigue had settled on her in a surprising way. In fact, she could hardly move.

With her cheek pressed into the pillow, she checked out the room. Walnut paneling covered the walls and the bedstead was made of polished tree branches woven together. A painting of a waterfall surrounded by a dense woodland hung above a mahogany chest of drawers.

She smiled because the style really appealed to her.

Rolling onto her side, she glanced at the large picture window. She had a view of treetops, a fading evening sky and a few stars just making an appearance.

She felt drugged out and tried to remember if she'd had anything to drink the night before. But she hadn't. She'd made love with Duncan high in the air then fallen asleep in his arms as he brought her back to earth.

She smiled happily and put a hand to her chest. She felt full and complete. Her hand drifted to her stomach and she winced. There was only one problem. Her nausea was back and just as her mouth filled with saliva, she pushed herself from bed, sprinted for the arched doorway, and stumbled into the bathroom.

She barely made it to the toilet when she threw up. And not just once, but repeatedly. She finally had to force her body to calm down because there was nothing in her stomach.

Sitting on the tile floor, she leaned against the side of the bathtub. The cast iron was cool against her skin.

She couldn't remember the last time she'd vomited. The stress of the past month must really be getting to her.

Queasy, faint, sore breasts.

And a vision of a child.

A strange white haze suddenly filled her mind. She didn't really want to think about anything right now except her need to keep moving forward with the black ops team. But the haze meant something, pointing her toward a couple of facts she didn't want to ponder.

Like why she'd thrown up.

Or why she'd been dizzy earlier when she'd first arrived at Duncan's cabin.

Or why her breasts hurt like they were on fire even now, though nothing was touching them.

No, she didn't want to think about these things. Not now. Not when she'd become a Warrior of the Blood and spent her nights killing death vampires and Third grid wreckers. Not when she served as the black ops team's shield.

But other realities intruded like the simple fact she now realized she'd missed her period.

She covered her face with her hands.

No, no, no.

This couldn't be happening, not to her, not in the middle of a war, not when she was about to go on a rescue mission to retrieve Merl's sister from Yolanthe's prison.

But her new reality wouldn't be denied as she recalled the vision of the dark-haired little girl calling Duncan 'Dad'.

Her hands fell away from her face. She stared at the open shelves opposite, at towels stacked up beside several bars of soap.

She was pregnant.

With Duncan's child.

And they were having a girl.

She focused on the Paradise Valley master bedroom and on the closet she'd stocked with new clothes. She mentally located jeans, underwear, and a soft violet cashmere sweater. She folded them onto the nearby bed then, while still sitting, she looked down at her tender, swollen breasts.

God help her, she was having a baby.

She rose slowly to her feet. As one in a dream, she turned the shower on and moved beneath a warm stream of water. She once again looked down at her breasts. They were definitely bigger, already preparing to nourish a child.

Moving her hands to her lower abdomen, she splayed her fingers over what would soon become swollen and full.

She was pregnant and she would be a mother, something she'd never expected.

Tears joined the streaming water as she let her emotions flow. She'd ignored the symptoms until now. On some level she must have known, but kept explaining away the nausea and the increased size of her breasts, as well as their painful tenderness.

She also knew a pregnancy would seriously complicate her life, her role on the ops team, and especially her relationship with Duncan.

She'd once asked him whether he ever thought about having children. His response still rang in her ears, sending a shard of fear into her heart. 'God no,' he'd said. 'What kind of father would I make with Carlyon as my example?'

She needed to tell him, though, right away. After getting dressed, she headed into the living area. This was not the kind of news she thought it would be wise to keep secret.

She saw him through the porch window and affection flowed through her in a swift wave. Was it truly possible she and Duncan would make a family together?

Duncan, she sent, but a strange kind of static returned and she knew something was wrong.

~ ~ ~

Duncan had his mug to his lips when a vision slammed into him. The heavy cup flew from his hands, bouncing down the steps of the porch. A powerful sense of urgency pummeled him hard and pushed him to his feet before he realized he'd even moved.

He couldn't see anything except the images in his head, so he threw his arms out to keep his balance.

A battle vision emerged of entering the darkening grid from the portal in Merl's home. Once inside, he began to run. Less than a minute later, wreckers arrived, at least two dozen of them, blasting through the grid wall.

Oh, God, so many.

The black ops team engaged them in battle. In the vision, they weren't shielded, though he didn't know why.

The vision skipped forward and he stood in front of Yolanthe's portal, part of the team with him, the other still fighting hard at the initial point of battle.

Within the vision, he accessed his wrist scanner and started to punch in the numbers to open Yolanthe's portal, then hesitated. He even asked Rachel to shield them, but she couldn't. She was being blocked.

At that point, the vision fell apart as though destroyed from somewhere in the future streams.

This sequence of events was a far cry from the original vision of finding Katlynn in a quiet prison.

He tried to access the vision again but it was shut down by some external force.

The only thing he knew for certain was the black ops team had to be inside the Third Earth darkening grid within the next five minutes or the woman and Merl's squad of What-Bees would be killed.

With his heart racing, he closed his eyes and contacted Luken telepathically, but there was no response. The seconds dragged by slowly. When Luken finally responded, a half minute had passed. *Who is this?*

Duncan.

I didn't get that. Who? There's interference of some kind.

Duncan shut the communication down.

Creator help him, what was he supposed to do now? He felt certain a Third Earth entity was disrupting not only the vision, but his ability to use his telepathy.

He calmed himself and thought about Merl and all the recent training. Within a few seconds, he knew what to do, but he had to act fast. He slipped his t-shirt off and ran down the steps of the porch onto a gravel path.

He began swelling his wing-locks and at the same time accessed his *grayle* power. Because of all the adrenaline in his system, his wings mounted the moment his *grayle* power came online and he was in flight. Somehow, the quick beat of his wings helped him to give full expression to his power.

He flapped hard, quickly breaching the forest canopy. He continued to fly then set his path in a slow circle. He focused on the strong *grayle* vibrations. But instead of only reaching out to Luken telepathically, he brought every member of the team fully within his mind, including

Rachel. Looking down, he saw that she now stood on the porch watching him.

When he knew he had everyone's telepathic attention, he sent, *Listen up, team. The vision of the future has changed. An unknown enemy has surfaced in the future streams and somehow impacted our rescue mission. Right now, we've got three minutes to get into the grid or we'll lose Katlynn and all seven of Merl's Third What-Bee squad. But this will mean battle against wrecker warriors, a lot of them. And Rachel won't be using her shielding power. And no, I don't know why except that she'll be blocked. But by whom or by what, I have no idea. And Merl, I'll need your wrist scanner. Everyone get to Militia HQ on the double.*

He didn't question for a second that they'd heard him, or that they'd respond to his directive, because he felt it. Closing the telepathy down, he drew his wings into close-mount and shot like a rocket back to the porch. He pulled up at the last second, landed on his feet, then in a smooth, Third-like manner, brought his wings into his locks.

Rachel had already changed into her battle suit, including her new dagger holster. "I'm ready."

Duncan waved a hand, donning his battle kilt and harness, silver studded wrist guards, battle sandals and shin guards. He put a hand on her shoulder and folded her to the Apache Junction Two landing platforms.

The officer on duty called out, "Luken left instructions. Fold straight to the Ops Cave."

Duncan dipped his chin, and with his hand on Rachel, folded both of them there.

To his astonishment, the entire team had already gathered, eyes wild with battle fervor. Endelle wore a red, cloud-like skirt with chain-mail beneath, the blade vest, black hip boots, and her horned helmet.

Merl handed him the wrist scanner and he snapped it on.

Merl then gathered everyone into a huddle. "Hands on each other's shoulders. We're doing a group fold to my home. I've already lit up the portal. Ready?"

~ ~ ~

Rachel had never felt anything like this in her life. The ramped up tension in the team flowed from person to person. She especially experienced the sensation where she touched Duncan's shoulder on one side and Luken's on the other.

"Now," Merl called out.

The trip through nether-space was a streak of power and a flash of energy. Within a split-second, they arrived in Merl's living room.

Merl addressed Duncan. "Which weapons did we use in your vision?"

"Wrecking shotguns and unidentified swords. Rachel threw her daggers."

Merl's eyes glinted. "You heard the man. Arm up."

Rachel wasn't sure why her shielding powers would be blocked, but right now it was more important to trust the vision.

Another blast of energy flowed over Rachel as the team acted as one. Weapons appeared in each hand.

Just as Merl had said, the portal was lit up in a soft glow and open to the grid.

"Inside now," Merl shouted.

Owen led the way since he was closest, and in the space of a few seconds everyone stood on the darkening grid floor. With a sudden snap, the portal closed.

Duncan took the lead and once more commanded the team's minds. *I'm heading in the direction of Yolanthe's portal. But we'll be meeting wreckers at a halfway point. The moment I raise my right closed fist, stop and turn to the grid wall off your left shoulders and prepare to do battle. Ready?*

An almost uniform response of 'yes' returned.

Rachel followed after Duncan as he ran swiftly through the grid. Joshua and Owen were on her heels, then Alex, Merl, and Luken. Endelle brought up the rear.

When Duncan began to slow, she watched for his signal. Sure enough his hand shot up and Rachel drew to a halt as did the rest of the team. Rumbling could be heard through the grid wall.

They'll be blasting through in five-four-three...

Though Rachel was ready with a dagger in each hand, her heart sounded like a drum inside her ears.

As each warrior raised shotguns, the rumbling reached a deafening point. At the same moment, a blast sounded on the other side of the grid and the darkening wall crumbled in front of the black ops team. All the warriors fired at a long line of wreckers, at least a dozen of them, with more coming. Most of them fell where they stood.

One warrior caught her eye and leaped from the grid, heading straight toward her. Clearly, he believed her a weak link. But without hesitation, she flipped her dagger and caught him in the throat. He dropped his sword and fell to his knees.

More wreckers came.

Moving to the back of the line and staying out of the way of battling swords, she drew a second blade. She scanned the encroaching Third Earth wreckers and found a target, one just emerging with a roar from the grid but leaping high into the air. She levitated swiftly, flicked her wrist, and the point of her blade hit his eye, piercing through to his brain. He fell.

She immediately resumed her position and continued pacing behind the battle.

At least another dozen wreckers emerged from the gaping hole in the grid wall. Some with shotguns, others with swords. They were fierce with three braids hanging on either sides of their faces, and wearing maroon battle harnesses. The wreckers leaped with loud shouts as each moved to attack the black ops line. She focused on those targets with shotguns and made each throw count.

The action was heaviest down at the end where Endelle, Luken, and Merl battled at least ten wreckers.

At the other end, Duncan battled with his sword as did Joshua, Owen, and Alex. The clanging of steel-on-steel reverberated in the tight space.

She threw a blade at a wrecker lifting his gun and brought him down. She then quickly slid two daggers from her belt, holding one in each hand.

She felt the movement of a fold behind her and spun as a wrecker appeared. She threw her first blade too quickly and caught the warrior in the shoulder. He grimaced as he pulled it out.

But his arrogance was his undoing since instead of either firing his shotgun or using his sword, he sneered at her. She shifted the second blade to her right hand and flicked it swiftly, catching him deep in his neck.

His eyes went wide. He clutched his throat, blood pouring from his mouth as he fell to the grid floor.

The battle had thinned in Duncan's direction when his telepathy, aimed at the entire team, hit her mind hard. *We've got less than two minutes to get to the portal.*

When he waved the team forward, she followed on his heels swiftly.

His telepathic voice arrived once more. *Endelle, do what you can to hold the rest off.*

You got it, came back from the woman who'd ruled Second Earth for millennia.

~ ~ ~

Endelle slipped through another fold just as Duncan and the forward portion of the team disappeared down the grid. She felt enlivened as though electricity vibrated through every cell of her body.

She saw the battle in slow-motion yet at the same time faster than ever. While within nether-space, she could see Luken and Merl grappling hard with several wreckers, each pushed to his limit.

The entire time she'd been fighting in the grid, she'd kept her peripheral vision fixed on Luken, guarding him with every ounce of energy she possessed. She spent at least half her time hidden within the nether-space of a fold so that she could surprise the enemy at just the right time.

So far, Luken had held his own against the Third Earth wreckers, his massive arms bulked with his phenomenal physical power. He was an Atlas among the vampires of Second and now Third Earth.

She re-materialized behind another wrecker, levitated to gain the right angle, and pierced him through the space below the collar bone, deep into his chest cavity. He fell where he stood.

She saw six more wreckers leap from the busted out wall of the darkening grid.

Shit.

The three of them now battled another dozen warriors and they had to get their asses to the portal. The darkening was an unpredictable mass of passages through time and space and the blasts of the wreckers had no doubt tipped the grid all on its own.

Just as she prepared to fold again, she saw her nightmare roll over on her. Luken had three wreckers in front and a fourth behind him. He'd be dead in a heartbeat, if she didn't get her righteous ass in gear.

Summoning her *grayle* power, she flew at the bastard behind him with her arms raised and her sword held aloft. She came down on his sword arm and took it off. The wrecker screamed, but Endelle didn't stop there. She allowed her forward momentum to catch him in the side, knocking him to the floor. In one quick movement she spun and brought her sword down on his neck, decapitating him.

We need to get out of here, she sent to Luken and Owen. *Duncan needs us at the portal now.*

138

We know, Luken returned.

She folded once more, coming up behind another wrecker and another. A few more seconds later and Owen brought the last of the wreckers down.

She contacted Duncan who immediately sent. *Fold to me now.*

Endelle locked onto Duncan's position, then grabbed both Luken and Owen, folding them to the rest of the team. The portal glowed a gold color, an indication the grid had locked in on Yolanthe's prison.

Yet for some reason, Duncan hesitated using the code she knew he possessed because of his original his vision.

"What are you waiting for?" Endelle called out.

~ ~ ~

Duncan stared at his wrist scanner, which had synced with Yolanthe's portal. But he couldn't act. Something didn't feel right or the future had changed yet again. He wasn't sure.

And before he could act, he had to know exactly what he was getting the team into.

Rachel, try to shield us. Something's wrong.

He shifted toward her and though he could see her *grayle* smoke as she attempted to access her shielding ability, nothing happened. "You were right; I'm being blocked somehow."

Duncan nodded. "All right. Let me figure this out."

~ ~ ~

Luken breathed hard as he stood between Endelle and Merl.

"What's he waiting for?" Endelle asked quietly. She side-stepped like a fighter, back and forth, ready to throw a punch.

"Ease down, Warrior," he said, catching her shoulder and pressing her in place, at least for a moment.

She glanced at him, nostrils flaring. She opened her mouth, probably intending to shout him down, but apparently thought the better of it.

She shook her head, and released more of her battle energy by dancing on the balls of her feet again. He didn't prevent her this time.

She was something else, this woman who'd lived as an ascended vampire for nine thousand years. And she had his back.

Thanks, he said.

She glanced at him with raised brows. *For what?*

For saving my ass. You think I didn't know I was done for back there? I knew a fourth wrecker was behind me, but with three swords in front, there was nothing I could do. Glad you're here.

At that, she grinned. *My pleasure, 'duhuro'.*

Luken returned her smile. 'Duhuro' was a word from the ancient language and a sign of great respect. *Back atcha.*

When the portal signal began to fade, Endelle growled. "All right. Get moving, Duncan."

But Luken caught her arm in a fierce grip. "This isn't your show. And you have to trust your team."

"Fine." She spit the word between gritted teeth.

Luken smiled. The woman was showing a tremendous amount of restraint given her unruly nature.

~ ~ ~

Duncan's heart raced. He'd lose the portal, but something within his mind or his body or both told him to wait.

He took a deep breath and gathered his *grayle* power once more then let it flood his mind. A vision shot through his head, this time sending ice shards through his veins because of the content.

He accessed his telepathy at the same time and shared what he saw with the team. *Yolanthe already has her forces in place opposite the portal, at least half a dozen shotguns aimed at the door, right now. So we've got a change of plans.*

At the right moment, we'll use our wrecking guns to blast a hole in the

Third grid wall. This will allow us to enter the prison several yards down the row of cells and avoid the ambush.

The presence of Yolanthe's Militia Warriors ready to do battle confirmed his belief that the earlier vision had been high-jacked by someone known to Yolanthe. The team's new placement would give them the advantage.

But a bigger problem presented itself — something so unexpected, he froze. His plan had involved making use of Yolanthe's portal to leave the prison and return to Second. However, as new images rolled, he saw something else entirely.

He had to share this reality with the team. He turned to face them all. "We've got a problem."

Lips parted, but no one said a word.

He explained about the need to shift their entry point, but their exit strategy would be a different matter. "Yolanthe's portal is different from Merl's; it shifts location, probably a security measure."

Merl called out. "That's exactly right. Only the wealthiest citizens have this kind of portal."

Every member of the team remained silent and he had no doubt each had just completed the sequence.

But it was Rachel who spoke the reality aloud. "We won't have a way to get back to Second."

She'd said it exactly right since none of them had access to the Grid from a Third Earth vantage point.

Were any of them prepared to take up a life on Third? And where the hell would they go once they rescued the prisoners?

He took a moment to gather his thoughts, looking the team over. He had a full minute before the timing was right to blow the prison grid wall. "We have a decision to make. Do we move forward or do we stay on Second?"

Owen, brows furrowed, spoke in a resonant voice, "We have people to rescue. Nothing else matters."

A murmured assent traveled the group.

Duncan dipped his chin. "Then we're all in agreement?"

A shout went up from each of the team members, a shared accord reminding Duncan why he loved the committed heart of the warrior as much as he did, male or female.

He turned around to face the grid wall.

He reverted to telepathy, his *grayle* power vibrating strongly in his chest. *We'll be about fifteen yards west of Yolanthe's Militia Warrior force. As soon as we bust down the wall, turn to your right and fire with shotguns, then attack with swords.*

He reloaded his shotgun and heard the others doing the same.

Aloud, he said, "On my mark." He could feel the team behind him, energy sparking from warrior to warrior. Rachel stood at his left. She'd spent the time at the portal folding dagger after dagger from the dead wreckers into her hands and wiping them down with a cloth from her dagger belt. Her sheaths were loaded once more.

Glancing at her, he said, "We'll need you in the back."

She obeyed his order instantly and moved to stand on Endelle's left.

When the vision neared the here-and-now, he shouted, "Fire up the shotguns. Here we go." As soon as his wing-power flowed down his shoulder and charged his weapon, he cried out, "Fire!"

Eight shotguns let loose and the darkening grid wall fell down.

Leading the way, Duncan saw the prisoners hanging from chains and staring at him. He immediately shifted to the right, turned, and let loose with the other barrel. The team moved into position firing as he had, lining up to face the enemy.

Yolanthe's warriors were caught unprepared. The front rows of warriors were blown to bits and fell back against those awaiting the black ops team in the wrong place. Setting his shotgun down, he advanced swiftly, sword aloft, a cry raging from his throat.

Joshua and Merl ran next to him on either side. Several of Yolanthe's warriors climbed over the bodies, swords in the air as well, two of them levitating.

With his *grayle* power in full force, Duncan folded and came up behind one warrior, slicing across his back. He arched and fell to the floor.

Duncan whirled and met a blade coming down hard. He blocked, leaned then delivered a hard punch to the ribs. His foe lost control of his sword as he reacted to the blow. Duncan slipped a dagger from his harness and drove it deep into his belly, pulling up at the same time.

The warrior went down.

He had no time to breathe as the next bastard levitated over Duncan. Holding his sword in both hands, Duncan kicked off with his back foot and slid low to swing his sword against the warrior's legs.

The shout of agony as the man came down, one leg partially severed, rang along the line of cells. Merl's What-Bee team, still in chains, roared their approval.

Yolanthe's warriors kept coming and Duncan folded once more and came up swinging.

~ ~ ~

In the relatively narrow hallway, Rachel remained deep in the background. Her dagger-throwing could easily catch one of her teammates, so she waited for an opening. Mostly she watched Endelle, who kept levitating and taunting Yolanthe's warriors, drawing those out who could levitate high into the air since the prison had a tall ceiling. Her costume lulled her male opponents into looking for a quick kill, but each met his death at her superior swordsmanship.

"Are you the one called Rachel?"

Rachel turned around. The sweet, melodious voice had to belong to the woman in the lavender veil who now stood pressed against her cell bars, trying to catch sight of the battle. She wouldn't have much luck since each cell had solid stone walls and the bars faced the opposite wall.

Rachel felt pulled in Katlynn's direction and moved to her. "I am. And you're Merl's sister, Katlynn, right?"

"Yes. Is Merl with you?" She peered down the hall. "I can't make out the warriors since the veil mars my sight just enough and the wall obscures the rest."

"Yes, Merl is here."

"Rachel, I need to tell you something. We're in trouble, all of us, even if your force wins the battle. There are things about the prison you can't know."

"Don't worry. We'll get the keys and free you as well as the men."

She shook her head, and because Rachel stood close enough to the cell, Katlynn caught her arm. "The chains the men use are charged. No one here is powerful enough to break apart the steel. And even if we could, none of us can fold from this prison, not you or Merl or any of the warriors he brought with him."

Rachel put a hand to her chest. "Oh, God." Had their rescue attempt become a trap?

Rachel noticed the damp spots on the woman's gown. "You've been weeping."

"From the time the team broke through. Yes."

"Is there no hope, because I can't believe it since we've been led here by vision after vision."

At that, Katlynn cocked her head. "You've had visions?"

"Not me. But Duncan has, several of them, all having to do with you."

"Duncan," she whispered. "He spoke to me telepathically." She turned away from the bars and put her hands on either side of her head. "This rescue was not of Merl's devising then?"

"Your brother's? No. The source, as I've said, came from Warrior Duncan. He's gifted with visions from the future streams."

Both the clanging of the chains in the cells and the shouts of the battle had begun to dim. Rachel glanced up the hall and saw that the black ops team had all but defeated Yolanthe's forces. Both Duncan and Joshua still battled, but it wouldn't be long now, and Owen and Merl were searching for the keys to the different cells.

Reverting her attention to Katlynn, Rachel took a step back. The woman had her hands outstretched and her head flung back. Her body glowed with a blue-green light and a similar smoke streamed from her body.

She had to be caught in some kind of vision herself.

When her light dimmed, Katlynn straightened her shoulders and lowered her arms. She then hurried in Rachel's direction and said in a terrified voice. "We have only a couple of minutes. I must touch 'the one' if we're going to escape."

"*The one?* You mean one of the men?"

"Yes, he is called 'The One'. I have spoken with my mistress. She says Yolanthe will come down here very soon and if she does, we're lost. Please find 'the one'. Hurry!"

Rachel blinked a couple of times, her heart pounding once more.

The One. Who the hell was 'the one'?

Both Endelle and Luken now spoke with the chained up warriors. Rachel reached for Luken telepathically and explained what was going on.

Luken glanced in the direction of Joshua and Duncan who had just defeated the last of the Militia Warriors. There was a terrible pile up of bodies at the entrance to the stairs.

Rachel had to look away. She'd gotten used to a lot of carnage in the past month, but she still had her moments, especially given the sensitive nature of her stomach.

Luken delivered a series of orders so that he, Duncan and Joshua came running in Katlynn's direction.

Rachel said, "I don't know which of the warriors she wants, but she says he's the only hope for getting all of us out alive." Her heart pounded once more.

""The One," Katlynn shouted. "He's called 'The One.'"

Duncan said, "Owen. She means Owen."

"Yes, The One."

Duncan's voice rang up the hall. "Owen, we need you. *Now.* And put some speed on. We've got trouble."

Owen came running over, his hazel eyes intense. Sweat dripped from his forehead, and blood spatter coated his uniform, arms and legs, like all the warriors. "What do you need?"

Rachel loved those words. She caught his arm and drew him close to Katlynn's cell. "Here's 'The One.'"

"Stand back, all of you," Katlynn shouted. "And prepare to fold."

"Fold where?" Luken asked.

For a moment, silence reigned. Rachel had no idea where they were supposed to go, nor did anyone else.

But Duncan's skin had developed a familiar soft glow and his *grayle* smoke streamed from his body. "I can see the place. We're to go to Phoenix Three, a hidden land."

Katlynn addressed Owen. "The One, put your hands in the cell and when I grip your arms, you must grip me back and not let go. But there will be pain."

Rachel, standing so close to Owen, watched him blink. "I'm yours to command." He slid his arms through and grabbed Katlynn's as well.

Rachel gasped and felt a powerful vibration begin to build within both Owen and Katlynn.

"Oh, shit," Luken said.

Rachel turned and slammed herself against Duncan. *We need to hunker down, get low. Tell your men. This is going to release some kind of energy surge.*

His telepathic voice reached the entire force at the same time, issuing the warning.

Whatever was going to happen, it would be enormous.

Chapter Nine

The future must unfold

In its own time.

Collected Proverbs – **Beatrice of Fourth**

Duncan pulled Rachel into his arms and pressed his back against the stone wall. He quickly slid to the floor as she clung to him. He could feel the power building in Katlynn's cell.

Suddenly, Yolanthe's voice penetrated his head. *Duncan, come to me.*

He turned and saw Yolanthe levitating above the dead bodies of her Militia Warriors. She wore sea-green silk, her lips as dark as he remembered, her pale blue eyes boring into his. He felt his hold on Rachel slacken, and he began to ease away from her.

Yolanthe floated in the air, coming toward him, arms outstretched. The compulsion to go to her took hold of him completely.

"Duncan!" Rachel shouted, grabbing his face with both hands, forcing him to turn back to her. "Look at me! Focus, warrior! Stay with me!"

Within his mind, he began forging a wall against Yolanthe. And just as he wrapped his arms around Rachel once more, a powerful blast of energy blew through the prison, emanating from Owen and Katlynn. Then another and another. If he and Rachel had been standing, they would have been thrown against the stone wall and possibly killed.

147

Another blast and the prison rocked from side-to-side.

Whatever Katlynn and Owen had created together could shift the earth.

When no more waves followed, he knew it was over.

He glanced up the hall and saw that Yolanthe had been knocked back to the stairwell and lay against one of her dead warriors, blood oozing from her mouth. His hope she'd been killed disappeared as she lifted her hand then moaned. She was badly injured, but he had no doubt she'd survive.

The next moment, the warriors in the cells were shouting to each other. Their doors were off the hinges and hung wide. He could see each warrior was free of his chains, though naked. They made their way swiftly to the hall.

One of them folded out of the prison, then returned. "Yolanthe's mist is gone. We're free."

As a group, all seven men went to where Merl now stood. The tallest warrior, a man with brown skin and black eyes, shoved at Merl with both hands. "You, bastard. You don't deserve to live." He then let his fist fly, hitting Merl hard on the chin.

Merl flew backward against the wall. Though he righted himself in a flash, no doubt ready to offer an explanation, his team vanished, folding out of the prison.

Rachel peeled herself off Duncan's lap and rose to her feet. Duncan joined her, his attention first ascertaining the team had survived then reverting to Katlynn and Owen.

Katlynn still held Owen's arms, but her veil was gone. She wore her brown hair in a crown of braids on top of her head. Her lips were parted as she stared at Owen. Tears glistened in her dark eyes.

Duncan moved in their direction and opened the door to Katlynn's cell. "We've got to get out of here."

But it was as though Katlynn couldn't hear. Instead of responding to Duncan, she remained close to Owen, gripping his arms through the bars of the cell clearly unwilling to let him go. Owen looked shell-shocked as he stared back at Katlynn.

Duncan knew they had less than a minute before Yolanthe recovered and began repairing the mist. He didn't have time to be subtle, so he slammed an arm down on their joined arms and shouted. "Stay and die, or leave with the rest of us."

This seemed to shake Owen out of his stupor. He pulled his arms away from Katlynn, but immediately went into the cell and simply picked her up in his arms. Duncan could feel the energy still vibrating through the couple because of what they'd just experienced and he definitely had his suspicions about their future.

The rest of the team had already moved in Duncan's direction.

"We're heading to Phoenix Three as a unit. I've seen where we're going, so let's link up, hands on shoulders and I'll get us all there."

As they'd done earlier as a team, each member made contact with the next until the circle was complete. With Yolanthe now sitting up and shrieking orders, he let his *grayle* power flow.

From the corner of his eye, he saw Yolanthe leap into the air, but she was too late. He merely smiled as he folded the team to Phoenix Three.

Because of the vision, Duncan was already prepared for the beauty of the new environment, but no one else.

Alex summed it up. "Phoenix Two never looked like this."

The fold had landed the team beside a smallish river and a nearby village. Cliffs rose at least three hundred feet on either side of the water, though the terrain stretched at least a half mile between. Children played at the edge of the river. Goats cried. A dog barked and a small boat floated with the current. A stone bridge connected the opposite bank where a breeze flowed over fields of produce.

Rachel drew close. "This is amazing. Is this really Phoenix Three?

"Yes, it is."

"Where's the desert?"

Duncan looked up. "At the top of those cliffs, I imagine."

A very tall man appeared suddenly, having folded ten feet from the team's position. "I see you made it, all nine of you. Well done. My name is Rex and I'm the creator of this hidden colony." He fixed his steely gaze on Duncan. "And I'm pleased to meet you at last, Warrior Duncan of Second Earth. Welcome to Third. We've been expecting you for a long time." He even extended his hand.

Duncan moved forward and took it. He felt immense power flow from Rex, like nothing he'd experienced before, not even with Endelle. Rex was definitely in her league, maybe higher, as though, like Endelle, he'd outgrown his dimension a long time ago.

Rex had thick, wavy black hair, warrior long, with several braids on either side of his face, though the mass was pulled back and worn in a loose clasp. He had a strong masculine look, very charismatic, with a thick nose, full lips, and broad cheekbones. His eyes were sharp and predatory, gray in color but with unique shards of brown mixed in.

He was also warrior big, carried a helluva lot of muscle, and had a woven black cape flung over his left shoulder. Taller than Warrior Medichi, Rex had to be at least six-eight. He wore black leather pants and beneath his cape, a vest tied with leather strings. He had on boots in the same material, hand-stitched, but of fine workmanship, and in a rugged style.

Duncan glanced around. "What is this place? This canyon? Nothing on Phoenix Two or One has a river like this."

"A hidden territory on Third Earth, a place I designed, carved out of the earth, and now protect with a veil of mist you probably can't see, despite your level of power."

His gaze slid past Duncan. "My Prime Seer has prophesied this moment for weeks now and we are tremendously overjoyed to have you here at last. She has sought each of you in the future streams and has prepared lodgings that would most suit you. Clothing has been provided and in an hour, I'd like you all to join me for a feast I've prepared in your honor. How does that sound?"

A murmured assent traveled the team.

Rex's gaze landed on Merl. "And don't worry. Your men are here as well, though at the far north end of the colony, twenty miles distant. You'll have ample time to explain all that transpired, so for now, be at ease."

Duncan glanced at Merl. Once arrived, Owen had relinquished his charge to Merl. The Third ascender had his arm around his sister, who in turn held tight to Merl's weapons harness despite the battle debris. Tear streamed down Katlynn's face.

Merl frowned. "But…you're Rex Vega."

"I am."

"We thought you long dead, as in centuries."

He shook his head. "I've been here, awaiting the arrival of the man who could locate Rapture's Edge." Having made this statement, all eyes turned toward Duncan.

Rex continued, as he met Duncan's gaze. "The fate of two worlds depends on your ability to find a place that until now, we've all believed belonged to our Third Earth fables."

Duncan nodded. "Though I won't pretend to be anything but astonished that my purpose is as you've said, I don't really have a sense of the place at all. I confess I'm mystified."

For some reason, this made Rex smile. "Just as you should be when you've been called to a purpose outside your wheelhouse. The future must unfold in its own time." His gaze then encompassed the entire group, "But, come. Take your ease in each dwelling assigned to you, get cleaned up, then we'll break bread together."

He turned and walked in his warrior stride back up a path laid with flat stones. Flowers lined the path and a woman rose up from a nearby vegetable garden and waved. "Welcome to Phoenix Three," she called out.

Several of the team thanked her for the warm greeting.

He felt Rachel's hand in his. Glancing at her, he watched as she glided her hand over her lower abdomen. Was she in pain? Had she gotten hurt?

But she smiled up at him, so maybe she was just feeling queasy again. "Do you see her garden, Duncan? She's growing watermelon in December, just as I did in Seattle One. I feel as though we've come to paradise. I think I could live here forever."

A profound wave of tenderness moved through him. God, he loved Rachel so much and it seemed the world he'd inadvertently brought her to suited her perfectly.

He was inclined to think she was right; Rex had created a paradise. But he wasn't sure he knew what to make of the man or the world he'd forged out of the desert. The river alone astonished him. How had the man put a river in a place like Phoenix, with woods in various places? He could even see a couple of smaller side canyons upstream.

Whatever the case, he felt oddly at home here as well, though he had no idea why.

~ ~ ~

As the team moved forward, Endelle hung back. She was on Third Earth in some kind of Rex-made wonderland, but she couldn't make her feet move. Her pulse throttled at top speed, she felt absurdly dizzy, and she had a bad feeling she knew the exact cause.

Rex.

Sweet dinosaurs and lords of all creation.

Rex.

The man was tall. She outstripped him in her stilettos, but not my much and if she lost her shoes, she'd have to reach up to wrap her arms around his neck. How awesome would that be?

But what the hell was she thinking? She'd just met the man and already she was wishing he'd lose the damn cape so she could get a better look at his ass in that fine black leather.

Something deep and hungry had come alive in her the moment she'd settled her gaze on his rugged, handsome face.

When the distance from the group made her look ridiculous, she levitated and caught up. She dropped down beside Luken, matching his long stride.

He winked at her. "That man's got some muscle on him."

"Hadn't noticed."

"Like hell. You're still slack-jawed."

She scowled at him. "Shut the fuck up. And don't forget that though you rule this team, I rule you."

But Luken only laughed.

From the moment she'd landed in Phoenix Three, her gaze had been fixed on Rex's left arm. It was completely bare and almost as big as Luken's. She supposed his right arm was a match, but how would she know since that same damn cape had also covered up his companion muscles. But she had a good imagination and it didn't take much to picture herself biting and sucking on all that hard flesh.

Ripples of bare-faced desire kept chasing other ripples down her arms, her back, and aiming like a rocket between her thighs.

"Just so ya know, Endelle," Luken said, keeping his voice low. "I think Braulio can go fuck himself for leaving you the way he did. Just sayin'. You've served your dimension way too long and those Sixth Earth assholes shouldn't have kept you chained to Second. Now you're on Third. I say, let your hair down."

Was he giving her permission to fuck the creator of Phoenix Three? "How about you keep your opinions to yourself for a change?"

"Again, just sayin'." He grinned, however, an expression that made her want to bitch-slap the team leader.

But Endelle knew she needed to be sensible, so she worked hard to keep her lust under control.

Over the next few minutes, Rex's servants led each of them to their respective dwellings. Much to Endelle's surprise, the tall man assigned to her folded her to an exotic house made of colorful stone walls. Several small, manmade waterfalls created a series of bathing pools and lounging areas in the front rooms. When she meandered toward the back of the house, she was absolutely stunned when she found a large room filled with at least twenty beautifully wrought outfits in a myriad of colors, and each in her basic overkill style.

Rex's Prime Seer had definitely done her homework.

The attached bathroom already had a tub full of bubbles waiting for her. She folded off her costume, letting it fall into a pile at the foot of the tub. She stepped in, sank beneath the foamy mass, and released a sigh so heavy it reverberated through the room.

The male servant entered at the same time, carrying a brass tray bearing a decanter of wine and a jewel studded goblet. He was also completely nude.

Her brows rose as her gaze landed on his impressive male apparatus, beautifully formed and hung.

He smiled. "I'm ready to serve you in whatever way you desire." He ran his index finger the length of his cock just in case she missed the point.

Her earlier lust for Rex rose in a heated flush to her cheeks. She wanted nothing more than to haul the servant into her bath, yet she hesitated. Some instinct warned her against taking him up on his offer. And that something had to do with a man wearing a cape and looking like a god.

"Though I am tempted, I'll just have the wine, thank you."

When he left, she slid her hand between her legs, fondling her swollen folds. With her free hand she sipped her wine, while her mind became intently focused on a very specific image of Rex's thick muscled arm.

~ ~ ~

Owen stood in the middle of a steel, glass, and leather living room, scowling. The decor suited him, which meant he'd been analyzed and he didn't like it one bit. He wanted everyone out of his business, not picking him apart and making decisions on his behalf.

He'd already sent the servant away; he could take care of himself.

He was irritated as hell and why wouldn't he be when fifteen minutes ago, he'd stood locked arm-to-arm with the veiled woman who had essentially blown the lid off his world. Literally.

The woman was Merl's sister, the one called Katlynn and he'd carried her through a fold to Phoenix Three, only relinquishing her when Merl called to her. She'd all but flown from Owen's arms and embraced her brother.

But the power. Oh, God, the power that had flowed through him, ripping apart everything he knew to be true about his life. His skin and his mind still buzzed with the aftereffects, holding him immobile even now.

Katlynn and her doe eyes, the sweet flowery perfume she wore, the soft peach bloom on her high cheekbones as she stared at him.

He hadn't really come back to himself since their shared power had set Merl's Third Earth What-Bee team free and momentarily destroyed Yolanthe's mist above the prison.

He wondered how long the disorientation would last.

He needed to get a move on. Rex wanted everyone back at his dining hall within the hour.

Finally, he forced his damn feet to move.

Heading to the massive stone shower, broad enough to mount his wings, he folded off his clothes, stepped in, and started scrubbing. He wanted Katlynn to see him at his best and not covered in battle blood. He wanted her to know he was a civilized man, even though he came from Second Earth to her advanced Third. He wanted her to know he was worthy, though every cell in his body knew the exact opposite to be true. He was ruined to the core when it came to women.

So, what the hell was he thinking anyway, worrying about her good opinion of him? He was caught in a war. What good would it do to be pursuing a woman on Third, when he didn't even know how long he'd be here?

Yet as he washed his hair, the shoulder length indicative of his in-between state, he felt a profound compulsion to get back to her. He also needed to see if Rex had a few extra weapons lying around. He'd already tried to fold his identified sword from Second Earth, but couldn't. Third was wrapped up tight as a drum and if he was going to make sure Katlynn stayed safe, he'd need some serious weaponry.

He was under no illusions about Rex's manmade paradise. Yolanthe of Mexico City Three now had several reasons to come after Duncan and the rest of the black ops team. And if what Duncan had said was accurate, someone in the future streams had started messing with him, someone no doubt in Yolanthe's employ, and who could possibly interfere with Rachel's shielding power.

When he was finally dressed, he was the first one to arrive at Rex's home. He positioned himself across the way near the river so he could see everything happening around him in a three-sixty.

If he wondered why he'd suddenly grown so concerned about a woman he'd just met, he set it down to the mysteries of ascended life. Whether he liked it or not, he felt in his gut he was intended to serve as the woman's bodyguard.

~ ~ ~

An hour later, when Luken arrived back at Rex's home, several of the warriors had already gone inside, including Owen who stuck close to Katlynn.

Luken didn't follow right away, but took a moment to have a good long look around. The temp in Phoenix Three was about perfect, even in December. He suspected a microclimate kept the entire canyon or valley, or whatever the hell this was, in a temperate state.

The palatial structure of Rex's home reminded him somewhat of

Endelle's McDowell Mountain palace, constructed as it was of cream-colored quarried stone.

When he finally entered the house, he saw that like Endelle's palace, Rex's home had no glass windows. The main living areas were open to the air, perfect for viewing what proved to be a mixed woodland, a sparkling river, and acres of cultivated ground.

Crossing through the main rooms, he found the team gathered around a massive dining table. For some reason, his gaze went to Endelle first and he noted the uneasy look in her eye. She blinked more than usual and kept glancing around the room as though afraid to let her gaze light on the man across from her and chatting with Duncan. He couldn't recall ever seeing Endelle knocked so completely out of stride.

But as he shifted his gaze to Rex, he could understand why.

The man had an undefinable quality, something so full of strength and power, even Endelle had to be awed. No doubt she'd gain her bearings soon enough, and give as good as she got. But for now, it was pleasant to watch her adrift, stunned like a rabbit caught in a snare.

She'd also toned down her wardrobe choice, wearing a single pheasant feather draped across a massive pile of her black curls and a multi-colored gown gathered at her left shoulder, the other one bare. Of course, heavy eye-make-up including gold sequins somehow pasted to the outside edge of each eye, gave her the usual over-the-top look. Still, she actually sat with her hands folded politely on her lap. Unbelievable.

As Luken looked around the table, he realized a chair was missing; there were too many guests and not enough places.

He was about to bring the oversight to one of the servant's attention, when Rex spread his hands and began speaking. "Now that we're all gathered, may I present my prime Seer, Megan of Atlanta Three." He gestured to a woman at the head of the table. "I've asked her to say the blessing."

The woman who rose to her feet had several blond braids looped on top of her head, though the bulk of her hair cascaded behind almost to her waist. She had a terrible scar across her right cheek angling to her lips and pulling up to distort her features. In the ascended world, scars occurred only two ways; if they were acquired before an ascension from Mortal Earth or if the individual wasn't allowed to self-heal. Luken wasn't sure why, but he suspected the latter.

Megan had an unusual inner spiritual light and seemed familiar in a way he couldn't explain as she lifted both her hands. Her eyes were a lovely green, her brows arched. Except for the twist of the scar, she must have been a beauty in her day.

When she spoke, her words were slightly twisted as well because of the scar. "Most blessed guests, you are welcome in Phoenix Three and our master, Rex, hopes you will stay among us as long as it pleases each of you. *Y pro nai-y-stae.*" Luken knew her words were from the ancient language and loosely meant 'stay forever'. Megan continued, "This night, pray be at ease and may the Creator bless this food to our use as we find nourishment at the master's table."

When she sat down, Luken immediately stood up. "Please, Rex, have my chair."

But Rex waved a hand. "Not needed. I have only one aim, to make sure you're all well-fed. I'll be directing traffic."

With that, he clapped his hands and a stream of servants arrived bearing bowls of steaming food and pitchers of what proved to be an excellent sangria.

As Luken sat down, he couldn't help but watch Endelle. She was slack-jawed again, no doubt because her host had proved not only to be charismatic but thoughtful as well. Her gaze rarely strayed from Rex as he took his time moving around the table, directing his wait staff and chatting with his guests.

Rachel and Duncan had their heads bent together. The new woman, Katlynn sat beside her brother, Merl. He held her hand and more than once palmed his cheeks in the same way Katlynn swiped at her tears.

The reunion of brother and sister had been a beautiful thing and had further helped Luken to forgive all of Merl's prior annoying behavior.

Owen sat on the other side of Katlynn. He had a similar expression as Endelle's and that's when Luken's heart sank. He'd been so busy battling and getting everyone to safety, he'd forgotten about the power surge that had allowed his team, as well as Merl's squad of What-Bees, to escape Yolanthe's home.

He suspected the *breh-hedden* had found its next victim, though time would tell. However, the fact Owen and Katlynn had created some kind of sonic boom to destroy a powerful veil of mist over Yolanthe's property seemed to indicate exactly how their relationship would progress.

He brought his goblet of sangria to his lips and set his gaze on a nearby bowl of cracked wheat salad. He'd been alone a long time and the presence of the *breh-hedden* hitting so many of his fellow warriors, yet skipping his own desert of a soul, made him wonder if he'd missed the boat somewhere along the way. Would he ever know the kind of bond many of his warrior friends had already experienced?

Luken. A faint female voice entered his head. He glanced at Endelle first, then Megan, Rachel and Katlynn in turn, wondering which of them had spoken to him. But each was engaged in conversation and couldn't have accessed his telepathy at the same time. Besides, the voice didn't sound familiar at all.

Who are you? He returned, focusing inward.

I'll be with you soon.

Are you here? In Phoenix Three? And again, who are you?

Nothing followed and he knew the unexpected communication had ended.

Great. Now another unknown entity had just entered the picture. But was she friend or foe?

~ ~ ~

Yolanthe lay on her *chaise-longue*, her back aching from having been slammed against the stone stairwell. She had a bump on her head as well as a variety of bruises, even a few cuts from flying debris.

The waves of energy created by Warrior Owen and Katlynn had stunned her in every way possible. If she'd ever believed the mousy female could have brought forth so much essential power, she would have killed her long ago.

She drew a deep breath. "I hurt," she whimpered.

Zander knelt beside her and pressed a cool cloth over her forehead. He'd summoned her favorite healer, but for some unknown reason the man hadn't yet come. She thought about killing him in place of Katlynn just to give some relief to her bashed sensibilities.

She still didn't understand how her careful plans had gone awry. Especially since Zander had finally made contact in the future streams with Duncan's brilliant presence of almost pure gold. Zander had seen Duncan and the team enter by her portal, so she'd set up the ambush with great care.

Zander had even found it possible to interfere when Duncan attempted to communicate telepathically with Warrior Luken. Of course, the moment Duncan had launched his *grayle* power, Zander's ability to disrupt Duncan had ended. But the biggest surprise was Zander's ability to prevent Rachel from using her shield in the Third grid. This alone gave her some hope for the future.

But above all, she greatly feared Duncan was finally coming to understand the scope of the power given to him. Every instinct screamed at her that she must find him, entrance him once more, then set him on his destined path to locate Rapture's Edge, solely on her behalf. Her window of opportunity was closing fast.

Only where the hell had he gone?

Zander had reentered the future streams very quickly following the debacle in her prison. But he'd found no sign of Duncan's stream, which meant he'd been blocked again, but by whom?

"I'm so sorry, sister. But I want you to know I won't give up." Zander took her hand in his and kissed her fingers.

"I know, dearest. I have every confidence in you."

Zander frowned suddenly. "Sister, I beg you to leave off your plans concerning Duncan. You were injured today and what would I do if anything happened to you?"

Her dear brother was so beautiful, just like their father. With her free hand, she caught his chin. "I will never leave you. I will always care for you."

"Yolanthe, please know that I don't need our father's love. He wanted me dead from the beginning and I truly have no feelings for him. I'm begging you to forget about Duncan and forego your plans."

She stared into silvery-blue eyes, loving her brother so much. "I do this because it's the right thing to do. You should have your inheritance and your rightful place in my father's home and in his plans for Second and Third Earth. Nothing less will answer."

He sighed heavily, no doubt understanding he wouldn't be able to move her from her path. More than anything else in the world, she wanted Zander to have his birthright. And she wouldn't let anything stop her, not even tonight's wretched outcome.

~ ~ ~

After dinner, Duncan walked with Rachel back to their dwelling. The serpent in his gut was quieter than he'd ever known it to be.

"Duncan, what is this place? Is it possible we all died in Yolanthe's prison and were transported to the afterlife?"

He chuckled. "I know what you mean. The Seer, Megan, did her research on each of us well."

Earlier, she'd led them personally to the home she'd prepared for them to share as a couple. Though they'd taken a tour of the dwelling, afterward they'd only had time to shower and change for the feast. But now they could explore the land surrounding the house as well.

He led her to a small vegetable patch, enclosed with a natural wood-branch fencing. Rachel opened the gate and moved inside.

He watched, leaning over the top rail of the fence. She was lit up from within, her love of gardening evident from the warm glow on her cheeks. She'd never looked more beautiful to him and a quick burst of *breh-hedden* desire streaked through his veins.

She rose up from examining a large plant and turned his direction. Her nostrils flared. "I can come back here later because I'm thinking you have something other than plowed earth on your mind."

The property was a half-mile from any other neighbor, so he said aloud, "Don't be so sure because I'm definitely thinking about ploughing."

Rachel laughed, moving toward the gate. "I'm coming."

"That's the idea."

Her laughing eyes met his as she sent. *You please me in every way and now I have a garden I can tend as well, time permitting.*

When she closed the gate behind her, Duncan took her hand. She'd been right to add the last bit about 'time permitting'. Every bone in his body knew Yolanthe would be out for blood and wouldn't rest until she'd made another attempt to bring him back under her control.

As he led Rachel up a rising path into a much narrower but wooded side canyon, he made an internal commitment to somehow end for good the woman's hold over him.

"You're tense, Duncan."

"I let my mind slip in Yolanthe's direction."

"Don't do that." But she chuckled. She knew him well.

He glanced at her, feeling eased just by her presence, by her laughter and the sparkle of her blue eyes.

She'd changed into jeans, a t-shirt, and tennis shoes and had let her long blond hair hang freely around her shoulders. He'd gotten rid of his battle gear as well, and now wore jeans as well. Yet he'd also found

a new stock of battle uniforms in the closet of the master bedroom. Megan had seen to all their needs.

He frowned for a moment as he thought of Megan. She seemed very familiar in a way he couldn't quite pin down, though he was honored that Rex's Prime Seer had been the one to see them to their home. At some point, he'd need a conversation with her about his suspicions that someone had interfered in the future streams. She might even know why Rachel hadn't been able to access her shielding ability while in the Third grid.

But not tonight. As he caught Rachel's garden scent, he wanted only one thing; to spend the next few hours with her and no one else.

The stream meandered through the side canyon, heading east to feed what Rex had named the Apache Falls River since there was a large waterfall at the north end of the colony. As Rex had explained at dinner, he'd fashioned the valley partly by design, and partly by exposing an underground river and several feeder streams. He'd done a lot of earth moving over a period of centuries.

As Duncan moved along the slight upward grade, a couple of smaller waterfalls spilled over boulders. Rachel exclaimed her pleasure more than once.

After a few minutes, he arrived at a small and very private grassy meadow.

Rachel drew up beside him. "This is so pretty." Purple wildflowers bloomed at the edge of the grass then gave way to more dense woodland. "Do you think this was deliberate?"

"Yes, I do."

"It would be a wonderful spot for a picnic."

He turned toward her and pulled her into his arms. *Or other things,* he sent. Without preamble, he kissed her and was rewarded with her eager body pressed up against his.

He deepened the kiss, driving his tongue in a steady rhythm.

When he drew back, he recalled a quilt hanging over the back of a chair in the master bedroom and folded it into his hand. Turning toward the lawn, he flipped it open and spread it out on the grass.

Rachel, always a willing partner, waved a hand and lost her clothes.

He groaned at the sight of her curves, her nipples peaked in the cool night air. He then returned the favor, shedding his jeans, shirt and shoes as well.

She dropped to the quilt, stretching out onto her back and holding her arms out for him.

"You look so beautiful, Rachel. More than ever. It's as though you seem happier to me. Is it this place?" He inclined his head in the direction of the wood and the stream.

Her lips parted and her eyes widened a little. He could see by her expression she was choosing her words carefully.

"What?" He smiled. "Are you keeping something from me?"

"No. That is, yes." As he knelt between her knees she gripped his arms. "There is something I've been wanting to talk to you about, but not yet. Is that okay?"

"You're asking a man if it's okay *not* to talk about something?"

At that, she chuckled, her eyes crinkling. "Right. You're all so anxious to open a vein."

His gaze slid to her throat. "Well, I am anxious to open your vein."

Her hands relaxed their grip and she let her arms fall above her head, her body undulating. "I want more than just your fangs right now."

He rubbed a hand down her abdomen and cupped her low. Easing his fingers inside her, he felt her moisture. He drove in and out a few times, loving the feel of her body clenching. She seemed different somehow, more ready for sex than ever, her skin glowing.

Something had changed with her, but he really was okay not to open that box just yet.

She continued to moan as he thrust his fingers in a steady rhythm.

But because her bonding scent was rich in his nostrils, he had to have more.

He took his fully erect cock in hand and positioned himself at her opening.

When he began to push, her body rolled and writhed once more. "I've needed this so much," she said, her voice hoarse, rich with need. "I can't seem to get enough of you these days."

"It's the *breh-hedden*."

Again, she looked at him with a speculative expression as she'd done moments ago. "Rachel, what is it?"

She released a deep sigh. "I need you to bite me."

When she turned her head, exposing her long pale throat, he forgot about everything else. Battling always made him hungry and as he curled his hips, driving into her between her legs, he dipped down to her neck and licked her throat.

Her warm, earthy scent brought a groan passing his lips while his fangs emerged. Angling himself, he bit in a quick strike and groaned once more as her blood hit his mouth.

As often happened when he drank from Rachel and when he made love to her at the same time, every vampire impulse that set the Upper Dimensions apart from Mortal Earth roared down on him. Pleasure flowed through his body, sending shivers over his heated skin.

She panted and moaned, uttering small cries that had his balls tightening. Nothing about his life was settled, not even where he lived or his relationship with Rachel. But making love with her and taking her life-force down his throat, made him feel more at home in his skin than at any other time before.

He sped up the movements of his hips and the push-pull of his cock. He sensed her pleasure rising to the pinnacle. *I want to come with you this time, Rachel.*

Yes, came back at him, a swift affirmative. Then, *Faster.*

Her blood powered him and as he suckled her vein, he sped up the drive of his cock, going vampire fast.

She let out a long keening cry as she began to come. His release swept through the hard length of his cock and he couldn't help but draw back from her throat and roar into the woodlands. Pleasure streaked like lightning, intense and pure.

She continued to cry out, over and over until at last the wave passed and his own pleasure gave way to a whole lot of feel-good.

He stayed connected and though supporting his weight with his forearms, rested his abdomen against hers.

She ran her fingers through his hair and sighed, then smiled, then sighed again.

He kissed her on the lips, each cheek in turn, her forehead, her neck, reveling in her presence in his life.

So much had changed for him, but would it be enough to quiet the serpent for good?

~ ~ ~

Rachel held Duncan's face in her hands and leaned up from the quilt to kiss him on the lips. He returned the kiss, pressing her back down. He was still buried inside her, a sensation she couldn't get enough of.

She'd wanted to tell him about the baby, but something within her held back so she went with it and kept her secret to herself.

She slid her arms around his shoulders and hugged him, wanting him to feel how much he meant to her. *We're on an extraordinary journey, aren't we?*

Yes, we are.

Even within her mind, his voice sounded deep and so masculine. They had an odd respite from the strange mission laid out for them, of finding the mythical place called Rapture's Edge, before Yolanthe or her father.

But for now, beneath a star-laden night sky, deep in a side canyon, near a wooded stream, she held him tight. She would make the most of these stolen hours until Duncan received a new vision and the next part of their mission arrived.

* * *

Stay tuned for episode 3 of Rapture's Edge, with the exciting conclusion of Rachel and Duncan's story and their search for Rapture's Edge. And with the same episode, enjoy the beginning of Owen and Katlynn's journey toward their Happily Ever After.

Caris Roane

Ascension Terminology

AAF pr. n. Allied Ascender Forces, Endelle's army.

ALA pr. n. Ascenders Liberation Army, the name Greaves assigned to his army.

ascender n. A mortal human of Earth who has moved permanently to the second dimension.

ascension n. The act of moving permanently from one dimension to a higher dimension.

ascendiate n. A mortal human who has answered the *call to* ascension and thereby commences his or her *rite of* ascension.

call of ascension n. A period of time, usually involving several weeks, in which the mortal human has experienced some or all of, but not limited to, the following: specific dreams about the next dimension, deep yearnings and longings of a soulful and inexplicable nature, visions of and possibly visits to any of the dimensional Borderlands, etc. See *Borderlands.*

ascension ceremony n. Upon the completion of the *rite of* ascension, the mortal undergoes a ceremony in which loyalty to the laws of Second Society are professed and the attributes of the vampire mantel along with immortality are bestowed.

answering the call to ascension n. The mortal human who experiences the hallmarks of the *call to ascension,* will at some point feel compelled to answer the *call to ascension* usually by demonstrating significant preternatural power.

call of ascension n. A period of time, usually involving several weeks, in which the mortal human has experienced some or all of, but not limited to, the following: specific dreams about the next dimension, deep yearnings and longings of a soulful and inexplicable nature, visions of and possibly visits to any of the dimensional Borderlands, etc. See *Borderlands*.

rite of ascension n. A three-day period during which time an *ascendiate* contemplates *ascending* to the next highest dimension.

the Borderlands pr. n. Those geographic areas that form dimensional borders at both ends of a dimensional pathway. The dimensional pathway is an access point through which travel can take place from one dimension to the next. See *Trough*.

breh-hedden n. (Term from an ancient language.) A mate-bonding ritual that can only be experienced by the most powerful warriors and the most powerful preternaturally gifted women. Effects of the *breh-hedden* can include but are not limited to: specific scent experience, extreme physical/sexual attraction, loss of rational thought, primal sexual drives, inexplicable need to bond, powerful need to experience deep *mind-engagement*, etc.

cadroen n. (Term from an ancient language.) The name for the hair clasp that holds back the ritual long hair of a Warrior of the Blood.

catch skin vb. When a blade draws blood.

Central pr.n. The office of the current administration that tracks movement of *death vampires* in both the second dimension and on *Mortal Earth* for the purpose of alerting the *Warriors of the Blood* and the *Militia Warriors* to illegal activities.

Command Center pr. n. Headquarters for the Allied Ascender Forces, currently at Endelle's Palace, Thorne's base of operations.

the darkening n. An area of *nether-space* that can be found during meditations and/or with strong preternatural darkening capabilities. Such abilities enable the *ascender* to move into nether-space and remain there or to use nether-space in order to be two places at once.

the darkening grid n. A grid built centuries ago, by powerful Third Earth entities that spans Second and Third Earth for the purpose of travel, transport, and access to Second Earth. The crossing of the dimensional boundary that allows access to a Lower Dimension, makes the grid highly illegal in the multiple-dimension arena.

darkening grid monitor n. A Third Earth specialist who tracks movement on the inter-dimensional darkening grid.

death vampire n. Any *vampire*, male or female, who partakes of *dying blood* automatically becomes a death vampire. Death vampires can have, but are not limited to, the following characteristics: remarkably increased physical strength, an increasingly porcelain complexion true of all ethnicities so that death vampires have a long-term reputation of looking very similar, a faint bluing of the porcelain complexion, increasing beauty of face, the ability to enthrall, the blackening of *wings* over a period of time. Though death vampires are not gender-specific, most are male. See *vampire*.

dimensional worlds n. Eleven thousand years ago, the first *ascender*, Luchianne, made the difficult transition from *Mortal Earth* to what became known as Second Earth. In the early millennia four more dimensions were discovered, Luchianne always leading the way. Each dimension's ascenders exhibited expanding preternatural power before ascension. Upper dimensions are generally closed off to the dimension or dimensions below. *See off-dimension*

duhuro n. (Term from an ancient language.) A word of respect which in the old language combines the spiritual offices of both servant and master. To call someone *duhuro* is to offer a profound compliment suggesting great worth.

dying blood n. Blood extracted from a mortal or an *ascender* at the point of death. This blood is highly addictive in nature. There is no known treatment for anyone who partakes of dying blood. The results of ingesting dying blood include, but are not limited to: increased physical, mental, or preternatural power, a sense of extreme euphoria, a deep sense of well-being, a sense of omnipotence and fearlessness, the taking in of the preternatural powers of the host body, etc. If dying blood is not taken on a regular basis, extreme abdominal cramps result without ceasing. Note: currently there is an antidote not for the addiction of dying blood itself but for the various results of ingesting dying blood. This means that a *death vampire* who drinks dying blood then partakes of the antidote will not show the usual physical side effects of ingesting dying blood; no whitening or faint bluing of the skin, no beautifying of features, no blackening of the *wings*, etc.

effetne n. (Term from an ancient language.) An expression, an intense form of supplication to the gods, an abasement of self, and of self-will.

folding v. Slang for dematerialization, since some believe that one does not actually dematerialize self or objects but rather one 'folds space' to move self or objects from one place to another. There is much scientific debate on this subject since at present neither theory can be proved.

grayle **n.** (Term from an ancient language.) The name for a misty power that only *Third Ascenders* possess. This power has two facets: a potent stream capable of taking life and a battling form that increases folding speed, levitation capacity, and physical power. *Grayle* is most often found among warriors.

grid n. The technology used by Central that allows for the tracking of *death vampires* primarily at the *Borderlands* on both *Mortal Earth* and Second Earth. Death vampires by nature carry a strong, traceable signal, unlike normal *vampires*. See *Central*.

Guardian of Ascension pr. n. A prestigious title and rank at present given only to those *Warriors of the Blood* who also serve to guard powerful *ascendiates* during their *rite of ascension*. In millennia past Guardians of Ascension were also those powerful ascenders who offered themselves in unique and powerful service to Second Society.

High Administrator pr. n. The designation given to a leader of a Second Earth *Territory*.

identified sword n. A sword made by Second Earth metallurgy that has the preternatural capacity to become identified to a single ascender. The identification process involves holding the sword by the grip for several continuous seconds. The identification of a sword to a single ascender means that only that person can touch or hold the sword. If anyone else tries to take possession of the sword, other than the owner, that person will die.

Militia Warrior pr. n. One of hundreds of thousands of warriors who serve Second Earth society as a policing force for the usual civic crimes and as a battling force, in squads only, to fight against the continual depredations of *death vampires* on both *Mortal Earth* and Second Earth.

millennial adjustment n. The phenomenon of time taking on a more fluid aspect with the passing of centuries.

mind-engagement n. The ability to penetrate another mind and experience the thoughts and memories of the other person. The ability to receive another mind and allow that person to experience one's thoughts and memories. These abilities must be present in order to complete the *breh-hedden*.

mist n. A preternatural creation designed to confuse the mind and thereby hide things or people. Most mortals and ascenders are unable to see mist. The powerful ascender, however is capable of seeing mist, which usually appears like an intricate mesh, or a cloud, or a web-like covering.

Mortal Earth pr. n The name for First Earth or the current modern world known simply as earth.

nether-space n. The unknowable regions of space. The space between dimensions is considered nether-space as well as the space found in *the darkening.*

off-dimension n. An expression referring to an ascender not being on his or her prime resident plant, e.g., an ascender from Second Earth who goes rogue and lives on Mortal Earth would be considered *off-dimension.*

pretty-boy n. Slang for *death vampire*, since most death vampires are male.

preternatural voyeurism n. The ability to 'open a window' with the power of the mind in order to see people and events happening elsewhere in real time. Two of the limits of preternatural voyeurism are: the voyeur must usually know the person or place and if the voyeur is engaged in darkening work, it is very difficult to make use of preternatural voyeurism at the same time.

royle **n.** (Term from an ancient language.) The literal translation is: a benevolent wind. More loosely translated, *royle* refers to the specific quality of having the capacity to create a state of benevolence, of good-will, within an entire people or culture. See *royle adj.*

royle adj. (Term from an ancient language.) This term is generally used to describe a specific coloration of wings: cream with three narrow bands at the outer tips of the wings when in full-span. The bands are always burnished gold, amethyst, and black. Because Luchianne, the first ascender and first vampire, had this coloration on her wings, anyone, therefore, whose wings matched Luchianne's was said to have *royle* wings. Having *royle* wings was considered a tremendous gift, holding great promise for the world.

Seer pr. n. An *ascender* gifted with the preternatural ability to ride the future streams and report on future events.

Seers Fortress pr. n. *Seers* have traditionally been gathered into compounds designed to provide a highly peaceful environment, thereby enhancing the *Seer's* ability to ride the future streams. The information gathered at a Seers Fortress benefits the local *High Administrator*. Some believe that the term *fortress* emerged as a protest to the prison-like conditions the *Seers* often have to endure.

spectacle n. The name given to events of gigantic proportion that include but are not limited to: trained squadrons of DNA altered geese, swans and ducks, ascenders with the specialized and dangerous skills of flight performance, intricate and often massive light and fireworks displays, as well as various forms of music.

Supreme High Administrator pr. n. The ruler of Second Earth. See *High Administrator*.

Territory pr. n. For the purpose of governance, Second Earth is divided up into groups of countries called Territories. Because the total population of Second Earth is only one percent of *Mortal Earth*, Territories were established as a simpler means of administering Second Society law. See *High Administrator*.

Trough pr. n. A slang term for a dimensional pathway. See *Borderlands*.

Twoling pr. n. Anyone born on Second Earth is a Twoling.

vampire n. The natural state of the *ascended* human. Every ascender is a vampire. The qualities of being a vampire include but are not limited to: immortality, the use of fangs to take blood, the use of fangs to release potent chemicals, increased physical power, increased preternatural ability, etc. Luchianne created the word *vampire* upon her *ascension* to Second Earth to identify in one word the totality of the changes she experienced upon that *ascension*. From the first, the taking of blood was viewed as an act of reverence and bonding, not as a means of death. The *Mortal Earth* myths surrounding the word *vampire* for the most part personify the Second Earth *death vampire*. See *death vampire*.

Warriors of the Blood pr. n. An elite fighting unit of usually seven powerful warriors, each with phenomenal preternatural ability and capable of battling several *death vampires* at any one time.

What-Bee pr. n. Slang for Warrior of the Blood, as in WOTB.

wings n. All *ascenders* eventually produce wings from wing-locks. Wing-lock is the term used to describe the apertures on the *ascender's* back from which the feathers and attending mesh-like superstructure emerge. Mounting wings involves a hormonal rush that some liken to sexual release. Flight is one of the finest experiences of ascended life. Wings can be held in a variety of positions including but not limited to: full-mount, close mount, aggressive mount, etc. Wings emerge over a period of time from one year to several hundred years. Wings can, but do not always, begin small in one decade then grow larger in later decades.

wrecker n. A warrior who serves to patrol the Third Earth *darkening grid* and destroy specific targets. Wreckers use identified, short-barrel shot-guns, with explosive cartridges, to bust through the darkening grid walls. Breaking up the grid walls shortens any distance through the grid. Grid monitors direct their paths.

y pro nai-y-stae **n.** (Term from an ancient language.) The loose translation is, *you may stay for an eternity.*

Thank you for reading Veiled: Rapture's Edge Book 2! In our new digital age, authors rely on readers more than ever to share the word. Here are some things you can do to help!

Sign up for my newsletter! You'll always have the *latest releases, hottest pics,* and *coolest contests!* **http://www.carisroane.com/contact-2/**

Leave a review! You've probably heard this a lot lately and wondered what the fuss is about. But reviews help your favorite authors -- A LOT -- to become visible to the digital reader. So, anytime you feel moved by a story, leave a short review at your favorite online retailer. And you don't have to be a blogger to do this, just a reader who loves books!

Enter my latest contest! I run contests all the time so be sure to check out my contest page today! ENTER NOW! **http://www.carisroane.com/contests/**

Coming Soon: Episode #3 of RAPTURE'S EDGE, the continuing saga of the Guardians of Ascension, again featuring Duncan and Rachel. Check out RAPTURE'S EDGE on my website. http://www.carisroane.com/raptures-edge/

Also Coming Soon: Book #8 of the Blood Rose Series, Mastyr Ian's story: EMBRACE THE HUNT!!! http://www.carisroane.com/the-blood-rose-series/

Also, be sure to check out the Blood Rose Tales – TRAPPED, HUNGER, and SEDUCED -- shorter works set in the world of the Blood Rose, for a quick, satisfying read.

BLOOD ROSE TALES BOX SET http://www.carisroane.com/blood-rose-tales-box-set/

About the Author

Caris Roane is the New York Times Bestselling author of over 75 books. Currently she writes paranormal romance. She began her career writing Regency romance for Kensington publishing and was awarded the prestigious Romantic Times Career Achievement Award in Regency Romance in 2005. Caris currently lives in Phoenix, Arizona with her two cats, Sebastien and Gizzy, and she really doesn't like scorpions at all!

www.carisroane.com

List of Books

To read more about each one, check out my books page: http://www.carisroane.com/books/

THE BLOOD ROSE SERIES:

EMBRACE THE DARK #1

EMBRACE THE MAGIC #2

EMBRACE THE MYSTERY #3

EMBRACE THE PASSION #4

EMBRACE THE NIGHT #5

EMBRACE THE WILD #6

EMBRACE THE WIND #7

Coming soon: EMBRACE THE HUNT

TO PURCHASE THE BLOOD ROSE TALES SEPARATELY:

TRAPPED

HUNGER

SEDUCED

Guardians of Ascension

ASCENSION

BURNING SKIES

WINGS OF FIRE

BORN OF ASHES

OBSIDIAN FLAME

GATES OF RAPTURE

Dawn of Ascension

BRINK OF ETERNITY

THE DARKENING

Rapture's Edge – Continuing the Guardians of Ascension

1 Awakening

2 Veiled

(Coming soon, book #3)

Amulet Series

WICKED NIGHT/DARK NIGHT (Boxed Set)

DARK NIGHT

WICKED NIGHT

Men in Chains Series (Complete)

BORN IN CHAINS

SAVAGE CHAINS

CHAINS OF DARKNESS

UNCHAINED

You can find me at:

Website: http://www.carisroane.com/

Blog: http://www.carisroane.com/journal/

Facebook:https://www.facebook.com/pages/Caris-Roane/160868114986060

Twitter: https://twitter.com/carisroane

Newsletter: http://www.carisroane.com/contact-2/

Pinterest: http://www.pinterest.com/carisroane/

Author of:

Guardians of Ascension Series (http://www.carisroane.com/the-guardians-of-ascension-series/) – **Warriors of the Blood crave the breh-hedden**

Dawn of Ascension Series (http://www.carisroane.com/dawn-of-ascension-series/) – **Militia Warriors battle to save Second Earth**

Rapture's Edge Series (http://www.carisroane.com/raptures-edge/) **(Part of Guardians of Ascension)** – **Second earth warriors travel to Third to save three dimensions from a tyrant's heinous ambitions**

Blood Rose Series (http://www.carisroane.com/the-blood-rose-series/) – **Only a blood rose can fulfill a mastyr vampire's deepest needs**

Blood Rose Tales (http://www.carisroane.com/blood-rose-tales-series/) – **Short tales of mastyr vampires who hunger to be satisfied**

Men in Chains Series (http://www.carisroane.com/men-in-chains-series/) – **Vampires struggling to get free of their chains and save the world**

CPSIA information can be obtained
at www.ICGtesting.com
Printed in the USA
FFOW04n1254080616
24858FF